Saving
SHILOH

Saving
SHILOH

by
**PHYLLIS
REYNOLDS
NAYLOR**

ALADDIN PAPERBACKS

Thanks to our friends, the Maddens,
of Friendly, West Virginia

First Aladdin Paperbacks edition February 1999
Copyright © 1997 by Phyllis Reynolds Naylor

Aladdin Paperbacks
An imprint of Simon & Schuster
Children's Publishing Division
1230 Avenue of the Americas
New York, NY 10020

Also available in an Atheneum Books for Young Readers hardcover edition.
Book design by Nina Barnett
The text of this book is set in Goudy

Printed and bound in the United States of America

20

The Library of Congress has cataloged the hardcover edition as follows:
Naylor, Phyllis Reynolds.
Saving Shiloh / Phyllis Reynolds Naylor.—1st ed.
p.   cm.
Sequel to: Shiloh season
Summary: Sixth-grader Marty and his family try to help their rough neighbor,
Judd Travers, change his mean ways, even though their West Virginia
community continues to expect the worst of him.
ISBN 0-689-81460-7
[1. Dogs—Fiction. 2. Family life—West Virginia—Fiction.
3. West Virginia—Fiction. 4. Prejudices—Fiction.] I. Title.
PZ7.N24Sav   1997
[Fic]—dc21
96-37373
ISBN 0-689-81461-5 (Aladdin pbk.)

To anyone who ever tried
to make a difference

One

There's one last thing to say about Shiloh before the story's over. I guess a dog's story ain't—isn't—ever over, even after he dies, 'cause if you lose a pet, you still go on loving him. But I couldn't bring myself to tell this part until now; of all the stuff that's happened, this was the scariest, and just thinking on it starts my hands to sweat.

When I first tried to get Shiloh from Judd Travers, who was treating that dog meaner than mud, at least there was a chance that if I couldn't have him for my own, Judd would let him live.

And even after Judd turns his beagle over to me, then starts drinkin' and talkin' ugly, there's hope he never meant it. But sometimes hope seems out of human hands entirely, and when the third thing happened . . . well, here's all that's left to tell.

Next to Christmas, I guess, Halloween is big in West

Virginia—out where we live, anyway, which is the little community of Shiloh, up the winding road from Friendly there on the Ohio River. It's because I first saw the little dog here in Shiloh that I named him what I did.

To get to our house, you go through this place called Little—you'll know it by the church—and you keep going along Middle Island Creek, wide as a river, till you see this old falling-down gristmill. It's right by this rusty bridge, and just over the bridge, you'll see the old Shiloh schoolhouse. SHILOH SCHOOL—1920–1957, reads a sign above the door, like a gravestone or something. I seen plenty of buildings got the date on them when they were built, but I never seen a building got the date when it died.

We live on the side of the creek near the mill, up the lane in a two-bedroom house. You sit out on the steps of an evening, don't move even your little finger, and pretty soon a buck will step out of the trees, a doe or two behind him, and parade across your field just as grand as you please. Now you tell me how many sixth-grade boys in the United States of America got somethin' like that to look on!

"What you going to be for Halloween next year, Marty?" asks Dara Lynn at supper. Halloween is over and gone, see, and already my skinny seven-year-old sister is thinkin' about the next. With her there's never no question. She dresses up like a witch every single year just so Ma can paint her fingernails black.

"I don't know," I tell her. "A ghoul, maybe."

"What's a ghoul?" asks Becky, who's three.

"Halfway between a ghost and a zombie," I say.

"Like a vampire?" asks Dara Lynn. Dara Lynn's big on vampires.

"Naw. Its skin is green, and it don't suck blood," I say.

2

"Marty!" Ma scolds, nodding toward my littlest sister.

We're having biscuits with sausage gravy for dinner, and there's nothing in the world I love more than sausage gravy. Except Shiloh, of course. And Shiloh loves that gravy, too, 'cause all through supper he's sittin' beside my chair with his muzzle on my leg, just waiting for me to finish up and pass that plate down to him so's he can lick up every last bit.

"I'm going to be a bunny," says Becky.

"Bunnies don't scare no one!" says Dara Lynn. "Why don't you be a pirate or something?"

"I don't *want* to scare no one," says Becky.

I guess there are *two* things I love more than sausage gravy: Shiloh and Becky.

Dad's washing up at the sink. We wait for him if we can, but sometimes his mail route takes longer than he thinks, and Becky gets hungry, so we eat.

"Passed by Sweeneys' house on the way home, and two of those straw men they rigged up on their porch have fallen over and been dragged out in the yard by their dogs," Dad says, sitting down at the table. "Look like a couple of drunks keeled over on the grass."

"Those straw men in overalls don't scare nobody," says Dara Lynn. "I want a dead man on our porch next Halloween with a face as white as flour."

"What's Shiloh going to be?" chirps Becky.

"He ain't going to be anything but his own self," I tell her. "Nobody messing with my dog."

"All this talk of Halloween, when Thanksgiving's right around the corner!" says Ma.

I guess there isn't that much to holler about where we live, so when a special day comes along, you want to hang on to it—keep Halloween stuff around till Christmas, and

Christmas lights goin' till Easter. I'm thinking how Ma wouldn't let us go trick-or-treating this year, though—not by ourselves.

"Houses too far apart for you kids to be walking out on the road," she'd said.

Well, the houses weren't any farther apart this year than last, and Dara Lynn and me went out then. But this time Dad drove us to the Halloween parade in Sistersville, and we had to do all our trick-or-treating there. I knew Ma was thinking of Judd Travers and the accident he'd had a month ago out on the road, drunk as he was. Knew she didn't want some other drunk to run his car into one of us.

Dara Lynn must have guessed what I'm thinking, 'cause she jokes, "We could always stuff Judd Travers and put him up on our porch. He'd scare off anybody."

"Hush," scolds Ma.

"There's enough talk going around about Judd Travers without you adding your two cents' worth," says Dad.

My ears prick up right quick. "What kind of talk?"

"None that makes one bit of sense," Dad tells me. "The man paid his fine for drunk driving, he busted up his leg and his truck besides, and as far as I can tell, he's trying to turn himself around. You'd think folks would want to help."

"I thought they were," I say. "Whelan's Garage fixed his truck up for him; people were takin' him groceries. . . ."

"That was when he was flat on his back, when he was really down. Now that he's on his feet again, there's the feeling around here that he got off way too easy. Heard Ed Sholt say as much down at the hardware store last week. Said we ought to keep Judd on the hot seat, let him know his kind wasn't wanted around here, and maybe he'd move somewhere else."

4

That sure would solve a lot of problems, I'm thinking. Ma wouldn't be so afraid for us kids out on the road, Dad wouldn't have to worry about Judd hunting up in our woods where a stray bullet could find its way down to our place, and I could rest easy that Judd wouldn't look for excuses to take Shiloh back; that he wouldn't hurt my dog out of spite, he ever got the chance. I think maybe I like the idea just fine.

"But what if he *doesn't* move?" says Ma. "What if everybody starts treatin' him worse'n dirt, and he stays right where he is?"

And suddenly I see a meaner Judd Travers than we ever saw before. Madder, too. I think how he used to kick Shiloh—even took a shot at the log where Shiloh and me were sitting once. A meaner Judd than that?

"Way I look at it," Dad goes on, "is that Judd's doing fine so far, and we ought to wait and see what happens."

Dara Lynn's got a mouth on her, though. "Ha! He's still got his leg in a cast," she says. "Get that cast off, and he'll be just as bad as before."

"Well, I believe in giving a man a second chance," Dad tells her.

"Beginning now," says Ma, fixing her eyes on us. "Your dad and I have talked about it, and we're inviting Judd here for Thanksgiving dinner."

Dara Lynn rolls her eyes and falls back in her chair. "Good-bye turkey!" she says, meaning she won't have no appetite come the fourth Thursday in November. As for me, I lose my appetite that very minute and set my plate on the floor.

Two

On the school bus next day, I tell David Howard who's coming to our house for Thanksgiving.

"Judd *Travers?*" he yells, and David's got a mouth bigger than Dara Lynn's. Every last person on that bus takes notice. "Why?"

"'Cause he don't have no other place to go," I mumble. All the kids are looking at me now.

"He'll probably show up drunk and drive right into your porch," says Fred Niles.

"He'll bring his gun and shoot your dog," says Sarah Peters.

Michael Sholt says, "If it was us, *my* dad wouldn't let him in the house! Judd was the one who knocked over our mailbox when he was drinking. And it was Dad who caught his black-and-white dog when somebody turned Judd's loose. Said it was almost as mean as Judd."

"He's just coming for dinner," I say. "It ain't like he's movin' in." I wish I'd never said anything. David Howard's my best friend, but he sure is loud.

In school, we're learning far more about Pilgrims than I ever wanted to know. All our spelling words for the last two weeks have had something to do with Pilgrims, so I have to learn words like "treaty," "colonist," "religious," and "celebration."

What I do like, though, is learning about the two Indians, Samoset and Squanto, who taught the Pilgrims how to plant corn. And how, except for the Indians, every single person who lives in the United States is either an immigrant himself or his great-granddaddy, maybe, came from a foreign country. Us Prestons are mostly English, a little Scotch and Irish thrown in. Miss Talbot says a lot of the early colonists were convicts, people who had been in jail in England, and were deported to America. I'll bet you anything Judd's great-great-great-great-granddaddy was somebody who'd been in jail.

Thanksgiving morning, I can smell the turkey roasting before I even open my eyes. We got a sixteen-pounder on sale, so Ma gets it in the oven early. I guess being hunkered down on a warm sofa, which is where I sleep, smelling turkey and knowing I don't have to go to school is about as close to heaven as I can get. Shiloh must think so, too. He's asleep against my feet, and every so often I can feel his paws twitch, like he's dreamin' of chasing rabbits.

Once Becky's awake, though, I don't sleep anymore, 'cause she'll come right over to the couch and stand with her face two inches from mine. She knows she's not supposed to wake me, so what she does is just stand there, her hot breath warming my eyelids. If I don't wake up right off, she'll start blowin' real soft—short little puffs—and then I know that whatever sleep I ain't had yet, I'm not gonna get.

I scoot over to one side so Becky can climb up and watch cartoons on TV. This morning, though, she's not content just to blow, her breath smelling of Cheerios and sleep; she's got to tap me on the cheek with the edge of the cardboard Pilgrim Dara Lynn brought home. I'm beginning to wish I'd never heard of Thanksgiving or Pilgrims, either one.

My job is to crack the bag of walnuts somebody give us so Ma can make a walnut pie—we always have us a walnut pie and pumpkin both. As soon as I'm dressed and get some cinnamon toast in me, I begin. Dara Lynn's settin' the table, putting little toothpick and marshmallow turkeys she's made by each plate. Dad slides the extra leaf in the table so there's room for Judd, and Shiloh just hangs around the kitchen, smelling that turkey. He don't know who's coming for dinner, and it's just as well.

Usually Ma sings when she's feeling good, but I notice she's not singing today. There's a frown-line that shows up on her forehead, and she bites her bottom lip as she tests the pie.

About two o'clock Dad says, "Well, I better drive over there and pick up Judd. Marty, why don't you come along?"

There's no reason I can think of why I should, but when Dad says that, it's 'cause he's got something to say to me. So I get my jacket.

I climb in the back of the Jeep. Judd, with his left leg in a cast, is going to need room up front to stretch himself out. As soon as we start down the lane, Dad says, "Now Marty, you being the oldest, Dara Lynn and Becky are going to take their cue from you. You treat Judd with respect, your sisters will learn a little something."

What's he think? I'm gonna start some kind of argument right there at the table? I don't respect Judd, but I can be polite.

"What I mean is," Dad goes on, "if he says something about Shiloh, don't go getting hot under the collar. Let's see if we can't get through this meal at least being good neighbors."

I want just as bad as anyone else to make peace with Judd, but there's one condition: "Long as you don't let him borrow Shiloh to go hunting," I say.

"Judd won't be doing any hunting this season, you can bet," says Dad. "He's got even more injuries besides that leg to heal up."

We reach the road, turn right a few yards, go around the big pothole that sent Judd's pickup truck rolling down the bank last month, then cross the bridge by the old mill. We turn right again and keep going till we get to the brown-and-white trailer where Judd lives.

He's already out in the yard, hobbling about on his cast and crutches. He's got brown hair, eyes that look smaller than they are on account of being so close together, and a mouth that don't seem to open as wide as it should, the words sliding out the corners when he speaks. Judd comes down the board walkway holding a gunnysack in one hand.

"Brought the missus a little somethin'," he says, sliding in after Dad leans over and opens the passenger door. He eases himself onto the seat—I'm wondering should I get out and help him—then pulls his crutches in after him, and rests the bag on his lap. Black walnuts, I figure.

9

"You seem to be getting around a little better," says Dad, making a U-turn and heading back toward the bridge.

"Doin' okay, but I'm still mighty sore," says Judd.

"How long you got to wear that cast?" I ask.

"Another month, I'm lucky. Longer, if I'm not."

I sure am glad to hear that—that he'll have that cast on all through deer season. There's only 'bout a week and a half of it left.

Middle Island Creek is on the other side of us now. Dad and Judd are talking about Judd's work at Whelan's Garage where he's a mechanic, and how wasn't it a good thing Whelan kept his job open for Judd while his bones heal— kept his job open and fixed up his truck, both. Then we're heading up the lane toward our house, and there's Shiloh standing out by the porch, tail going back and forth, his rear end doing this little welcoming dance.

But suddenly his dancing stops, tail goes between his legs, and he's up on the porch, whining to get in. Don't take no genius to know he's got a whiff or a look or both of Judd Travers, and is scared the man's come to take him back. I wouldn't let that dog go to save my life.

Ma opens the door for Shiloh, then comes out herself. "Happy Thanksgiving, Judd," she says, and when she smiles, she's got this dimple in one cheek. "I got dinner on the table. Hope you're hungry."

Judd thunks up the steps and hands Ma the gunnysack. "Brought you somethin'," he says.

Becky and Dara Lynn are hangin' back by the door, but they get wind there's a present, they're right out there, tryin' to see in the bag.

"Why, thank you, Judd," says Ma. She opens the sack and starts to put one hand in, then draws it out real quick.

"Eeeuuu!" cries Dara Lynn, getting herself a look. "What is it?"

"Squirrel," says Judd, mighty proud of himself. "They're already bled. Woulda skinned 'em, too, if I'd had the time, but I shot 'em not long before Ray come over."

I see now where the blood's stained one side of the gunnysack.

"Those'll make a fine-tasting stew," says Dad, and he takes the bag himself and sets it on the porch. "I'll skin these after dinner." And then, "Didn't know you could hunt with that leg like it is."

Judd laughs. "Not much hunting to it. I just picked those squirrels off while I was sittin' on my front steps." And he follows my folks inside.

I'm feeling sick at my stomach. I'm remembering how David Howard and me were over at Judd's once, before the accident, and saw him shoot a squirrel just for the pure mean joy of it. Didn't even cook it, just threw it to his dogs.

"Well," says Ma. "Guess we can all sit down at the table, if you're ready."

Becky takes the long way around the kitchen so she don't have to get within four feet of Judd. Shiloh's nowhere to be found; usually he'd have his nose right at the edge of the table, waiting for a piece of that turkey to stand up and walk his way.

It sure ain't—isn't—what you'd call a comfortable Thanksgiving. About the way the Pilgrims must have felt with Indians there. Or maybe the way Samoset and Squanto felt with the Pilgrims—everybody a little too polite.

Ma usually has us do somethin' special on Thanksgiving. Like last year, we each had to think up three things we were thankful for, and the year before that, we had to say something nice about the person on our right, except that Becky couldn't talk yet, and the person on *my* right was Dara Lynn. Only nice thing I could think to say about her was that she didn't look too bad with three teeth missin'.

This year, though, with Judd there, Dad offers the prayer he usually prays on Sundays. He thanks God for the food before us and says, "Bless it to nourish our good. Amen." Dara Lynn don't even bow her head, she's so afraid somebody's going to get the drumstick she's set her eye on.

Everyone smiles when the prayin's over, and Ma says, "Now Judd, you just help yourself to whatever you see before you, and we'll start the platters around. I've sliced some white meat and dark meat both." And the eatin' begins.

With all that food coming at me, I almost forget for a time that we got Judd to look at across the table, but once we get a little in our bellies, I can see the conversation isn't going very far.

First off, Judd's embarrassed. I think he likes the food, all right, but he don't especially like being at our table. It's like he owes us somethin' for finding him after his accident, and Judd don't like to owe nobody nothing. Guess he figured if he was to refuse our invitation, though, it'd be like a slap in the face. And bad as he is, even he's got a limit to rudeness. I look across at him, shoveling that food in like the sooner he gets it down the sooner he can leave, and I'm tryin' to think of a question to ask that'll give everybody a chance to say somethin'.

But right that minute Becky says, "What was the turkey's name?"

We all look at her.

"Only pet turkeys have names, Becky," Dad says. "We bought this turkey at the store."

That gives Judd something to talk about. "I got me a fine wild turkey last year. Bought one of those turkey callers, and after I got the hang of it, I bagged a thirteen-pounder."

Dara Lynn's thinkin' that over. "You make a call like a turkey, and when a real one shows up, you blow its head off?"

"That's about it," says Judd.

Ma never looks up—just goes on cutting her meat, her cheeks pink—but Becky stops chewing her turkey wing and she is glaring at Judd something awful. Boy, you get a three-year-old girl lookin' at you that way, she's got a scowl would stop a clock.

I'm just about to ask Ma to pass the sweet potatoes when I hear Becky say, "We'll blow *your* head off!" and suddenly there is quiet around that table you wouldn't believe.

Three

Well, Thanksgiving sure went downhill after that. You wouldn't think a three-year-old could say anything that would cause much trouble, but it just seemed to put into words the feeling we had about Judd Travers.

Judd looks over at Becky and says, a little sharp-like, "Hey, little gal, you ain't havin' much trouble eatin' that turkey, I see. Somebody had to kill that."

Becky looks at the turkey wing and slowly lowers it onto her plate, then turns her scowl toward Judd again, her bottom lip stickin' out so far you could hang a bucket on it.

Everybody starts talkin' at once. Ma asks wouldn't Judd like some more gravy, and Dad wants to know if he's going to watch the football game that afternoon, but their voices seem too loud and high. By the time Ma cuts the pie, we don't have much taste for it. I don't, anyway. Judd eats one piece of pumpkin, and Ma says she'll send a piece of the walnut home with him. Then her cheeks turn pink again, 'cause it sounds like maybe she can't wait for him to go, and she says, "But of course you're staying to watch the game, aren't you?"

Judd don't say yes or no, but when Dad turns on the TV, the picture's fuzzy on account of we don't have us a satellite dish. Judd's got one in his yard that's bigger'n his trailer, almost. And that gives him a real fine excuse to say no, he thinks he'll go on home, prop up his leg, and watch the game there.

Now that he's leavin', we're all smiles and politeness, standing around waiting for Judd to get his jacket on.

"Where's that dog of yours?" Judd says to me, pulling his sleeve down over the cuff of his shirt. That's about the first time he ever admitted that Shiloh was really mine.

I decide Shiloh's gonna say good-bye if I have to drag him out, and I do. I go behind the couch where he's lyin', about as far back in the corner as he can get, and I have to take two of his paws and tug. He's shaking already, but I hold him tight so he'll know he belongs to me.

Judd looks him over. "Shyest dog I ever seen," he says. But again, just like he did when we went to visit him after the accident, Judd puts out his hand and strokes Shiloh on the head. He's still awkward about it, but he's learnin'. It was Shiloh who barked when Judd's pickup rolled down the bank, really Shiloh who saved his life, and Judd knows that. And once more, Shiloh licks his hand. It's a feeble sort of lick, but Judd likes it, I can tell. I figure Judd's a person who don't get no kisses and hugs from anyone.

After Dad and Judd get in the Jeep, Ma moves about the kitchen, her lips pressed together like she's seen better Thanksgivings, so Becky and Dara Lynn make themselves scarce. They go in the next room and gather up all the Thanksgiving cutouts Dara Lynn brought home from school. They make like they're paper dolls, the Pilgrims riding around on the big cardboard turkey, and the Indians sittin' on this pumpkin.

When Dad gets back, though, he takes out after me! I can't believe it!

"Marty, you didn't say more'n five words to Judd the whole time he was here."

I bet I said fifty, maybe, but I'll admit, I didn't say a whole lot. "What're you yellin' at me for?" I ask. "It's Becky you should be scolding for sayin' too much."

He knows it and I know it, but truth is, you can't hardly scold a three-year-old girl for anything, and Dad would rather cut off his thumb than make Becky cry.

Then Ma chimes in: "Marty's right, Ray. Don't take it out on him."

Dad turns on her then: "Why do you always side with Marty? We have a guest for dinner, I expect everyone to pitch in and be sociable. Can't me be doing all the talking."

I know he's not really mad at Ma, either. He just wishes the day had gone better—we was all so stiff.

But that's enough to set Ma off. "Well, if you want to stand out here in the kitchen and do all the cooking next time, *I'll* sit in the other room and talk. How about that?"

Oh boy, this is the worst Thanksgiving I can remember. Dad turns on the TV to watch the game, then turns it off again, picture's so bad. Becky's leaning over a sofa cushion, sucking her thumb and twisting a lock of hair—ready for a nap.

And then I realize that not a single word's been aimed at Dara Lynn. If *she* had opened her mouth, no telling *what* would've come out; she can sass the ears off a mule. How come *she* got through Thanksgiving without even a look? I find myself gettin' all churned up inside, and when she comes out of the kitchen with the wishbone—the Thanksgiving turkey *wish*bone—and asks Becky to pull it with her, it's all I can do not to reach out and sock her arm.

"Make a wish, Becky, then pull," she says.

This ain't no fair contest, 'cause Dara Lynn's holding that wishbone right close to the top, and Becky's little hand hardly has a grip on it. Guess who wins.

"I got the center, so now you got to tell your wish," Dara Lynn crows.

Becky stands there looking at the broken wishbone in her hand and starts to cry.

"It's *supposed* to break, Becky!" Dara Lynn says, but Becky goes on bawling, and finally Dad snaps at Dara Lynn. Nicest thing that's happened all day.

I hate it when Ma and Dad aren't talking, though—feel all tight inside. Shiloh feels the same say, I can tell. Lies down on his belly with his head on his paws, his big brown eyes travelin' back and forth from Ma to Dad. Every so often, when their voices get extra sharp, his ears will twitch. But that evening, after we have us some turkey sandwiches, Dad says to Ma, "Why don't you go put your feet up, and Marty and I will make stew out of that squirrel meat."

Last thing in this world I want to do, but I put on my jacket and go out on the porch with Dad. He shows me how you skin a squirrel by cutting a ring around the back legs at the feet, then around the top of the base of the tail. He lays the squirrel on its back, puts his foot on its tail, grabs its back legs and pulls, and the skin comes off like a jacket, right up to the neck. I think I am going to throw up.

"You get the other two done, you call me," I say, and go

17

back inside. Why Judd Travers would bring over three dead squirrels as a present to my ma, I don't have a clue. But the thing is, Dad's a hunter, too, so I got to be real careful what I say. When he comes back in, he's cut off the heads, the back feet, and the tails of those squirrels, he's gutted them, and now we got to soak them. I fill a pan with water.

It's later, after Ma's put Becky to bed and is reading a story to Dara Lynn, that Dad and me cut up the squirrel meat. I feel like a murderer.

"I don't think I want any of this after it's cooked," I say finally.

"Nobody's going to make you eat it," says Dad.

"Bet I could be a vegetarian," I say. "I could live just fine on corn and beans and potatoes."

"For about a week, maybe," Dad tells me. "You'd be first to complain."

"Would not!" I say. "I just can't see going hunting. I can't see how you can shoot a deer or a rabbit or anything." I sure am getting smart in the mouth, I know that.

Dad's voice has an edge to it. "You like fried chicken, don't you? Like a good piece of pot roast now and then?"

I think about all I'd have to give up if I gave up meat. Forgot about fried chicken.

"Judd was right about one thing," Dad goes on. "Just because we didn't kill the meat we get from the store don't mean it died a natural death. The hamburger you eat was once a steer, don't forget. Somebody had to raise that steer, send it to market, and someone else had to slaughter it— just so's you could have a hamburger."

I'd have to give up hamburgers, too? I'm quiet a long time trying to figure things out. "Well, if I wanted to be a vegetarian, could I?"

Dad thinks on this awhile as he drops the meat in a pot of water he's got boiling on the back of the stove. "Suppose you could. But of course you'd have to get rid of that cowboy hat I bought you at the rodeo. Your belt, too."

"Why?" I say.

"They're leather; it's only fair. You don't want animals killed for their meat, then I figure you don't want 'em killed for their hide, either. And you know those boots you had your eye on over in Middlebourne? You can forget those, too. Same as that vest you got last year at Christmas, the suede one with the fringe around the bottom."

Man oh man, life is more complicated than I thought. One decision after another, and no matter which way you lean, there's an argument against it. What it comes down to is that I like to eat meat if I don't have to know how the animal died. And I sure don't want to give up my rodeo hat.

"Well, one thing I know," I tell my dad as we set to work cutting up the potatoes and carrots, "I don't want Shiloh turned into a hunting dog."

Dad don't answer right off, but I can tell by the way he's chopping that I struck a nerve. "He was already a hunting dog before you got him," he says. "I was hoping I could take him coon hunting with me some night."

"He's not going to be no hunting dog!" I say louder.

"Well, he belongs to you, Marty. You got the right to say no, I guess." And then, after we put the vegetables in the fridge, waiting to go in the pot when the meat's tender, Dad says, "Tomorrow, I want you to take some of this stew over to Judd, and thank him for the squirrels."

I figure this is my punishment, and maybe I had it coming.

Four

When I get up next morning, Ma's got this big waffle sittin' on my plate, a sausage alongside it, little pools of yellow margarine melting in the squares. Syrup's hot, too.

Still, a waffle can't make up for the fact that on a day off school, wind blowin' like crazy, I got to hike over to Judd's place and give him the remains of what I wish he hadn't shot in the first place.

To make things worse, Dara Lynn's sittin' across from me in her Minnie Mouse pajamas and, knowin' I got to go to Judd's, crows, "I'm not gonna go outside alllll day! I'm just gonna sit in this warm house and play with my paper dolls." And when that don't get a rise out of me, she adds, "Alllll day! I don't have to go nowhere."

I asked Ma once if Dara Lynn had been born into our family by accident or on purpose, and she said that wasn't the kind of question you should ask about anyone.

Accident, I'm thinkin', looking at her now. Nobody'd have a daughter like that on purpose.

Shiloh starts dancin' around when I put on my jacket and cap. He thinks we're going to take a run down to Doc Murphy's or somethin', but I know that as soon as I turn right at the end of the lane, he'll start to whine and go back. Surprises me, though. This time he goes halfway across the bridge before he stops. I finish the rest of the trip alone.

I'm thinkin' how when a man wrecks his truck and his leg both, and almost loses his job—his life, even—he's sunk about as low as he can get. Dad says either he'll hate himself so much he'll decide to change, or he'll hate the way other folks feel about him, and turn that hating onto them. Sure hope he don't turn his hating onto me.

I'm passing by the house of one of Judd's neighbors, the family that took two of his dogs to care for till Judd's better. I see the smaller one at their window now, barkin' at me, but his tail's wagging. Never saw any of Judd's dogs wag their tails before.

I get to Judd's and have to knock three times before he comes to the door, and then I see I woke him up.

"What you doin' out this early?" he asks, hair hangin' down over his face, his pants pulled on over a pair of boxer shorts bunched up above his waistband.

"Dad wanted me to bring over this squirrel stew," I tell him, handing him the jar. "Thought you ought to have a share of it."

That pleases him then—as much as you can please a man you just woke up. "Can get some more squirrels where those come from—pick 'em right off the tree," he says, and laughs.

It's then I know this is one big mistake.

"Well," I say, "actually, we don't eat all that much meat. But Ma didn't want the stew to go to waste." Trying to be polite and honest at the same time is hard work.

Judd quits smilin'. "She *didn't* like it then, so you're giving it to me?"

Uh-oh. "No! She likes it fine. Just wanted you to have some." Right this minute I am wondering what the difference is between a fib and a lie. Last summer, when Shiloh run away from Judd and come to me, and I hid him up in our woods, I told Judd Travers I hadn't seen his dog. Didn't tell my folks I had Shiloh, neither, and they claim I lied. What am I doing now? I'd like to know. Ma don't appreciate those dead squirrels any more than I do. If I stand here and tell Judd Travers the naked truth, though, I'll get my britches warmed pretty quick when I get home, you can bet.

"Well, you tell your ma that anytime she wants some more, let me know. I can't hunt nothing else, I can at least shoot squirrel."

"I'll tell her," I say. And I head back home.

There's somethin' good waiting for me when I get there. Ma says David Howard called and wants to know can I spend the day at his place. His ma will be picking me up about eleven.

"Ya-hoo!" I say, throwing my jacket in the air, and Shiloh dances around, too; if there's any happiness going on, he's a part of it.

"Change your shirt and comb your hair," says Ma.

I go into the girls' bedroom where I got a bureau in the corner, all my clothes in it. I get out a sweatshirt with BLACKWATER FALLS on it, and put it on.

Dara Lynn's still in her pajamas—she and Becky. Got their paper dolls spread all over the bed.

22

"Where *you* goin'?" Dara Lynn asks.

"Over to David's," I say. And then, not even looking at her, "Can't wait to have lunch at David Howard's: chicken salad with pineapple in it, pickles and potato chips, and a big old fudge brownie covered with coffee ice cream and chocolate sauce." Truth is, I don't know what we're havin' for lunch, but figure that's close.

Now I done it. Dara Lynn slides off the bed and goes hollerin' out to the kitchen to ask why don't we never have fudge brownies and chocolate sauce, and I get away just in time.

David's in the car with his mother when they pull in. For the second time that day, Shiloh thinks he's going somewhere, but don't even get out of the house. I give him a hug and tell him we'll have a run when I get home, and then I slide in the backseat beside David. Since we usually play up in David's room, his ma don't appreciate a dog runnin' around inside the house.

"How was Thanksgiving, Marty?" she asks. Mrs. Howard's got blond hair, and she's wearin' a heavy white sweater. She teaches high school. David's dad works for the *Tyler Star–News*.

"Yeah," says David. "How was dinner with Judd?"

"Nothing special," I say. "It was okay."

"Was he drunk?"

"'Course not, but he's still banged up pretty bad. He'll be wearing that cast another month, at least."

"Do you see any change in him, Marty?" asks Mrs. Howard, and I can tell by her voice she don't expect much.

"Not a lot, but Dad says he's tryin'," I answer.

David and me each tell what all we ate on Thanksgiving—how many rolls and helpings of stuffing, and after the car goes back down the winding road, through Little, and past the post office in Friendly, we get to David's house, which is two stories high (four, counting the attic and basement), and has a porch that wraps around three sides of it.

David whispers he has a secret but won't tell me till we're in his room, so while his mom gets lunch, we go upstairs. David's room has a map of the universe on one wall and a globe on his bookcase. Except for the bunk beds, David Howard's bedroom looks like a school. Got his own desk and chair, bulletin board, and encyclopedias.

As soon as we're alone, he closes the door. "Guess what? You know that fight Judd Travers was in, back before his accident?"

"Yeah?" I say. "With the guy from Bens Run?"

"Yes," says David. "Well, the man's missing. It's going to be in the newspaper this week."

"So?" I say. "What's Judd got to do with it? He's been laid up for weeks now with that broken leg."

David's eyes gleam like two small penlights. "The man's been missing since *before* Judd's accident. His family just now reported it. What do you bet Judd killed him?"

"*What?*"

"I think Judd was trying to wreck the evidence along with his truck."

"Go on!" I say. "And maybe kill himself in the bargain? You're nuts!"

"Marty, we've got to check it out! I'll bet we'd find blood on the seat or something." David gets excited about somethin', he almost shoots off sparks.

"If there's blood on the seat, it's Judd's," I tell him.

David shakes his head. "Here's how I figure: Judd and the man from Bens Run had another fight, and Judd kills him. Maybe he didn't mean to, but he did. Throws the body into the cab of his pickup to hide it, then buries it and tries to rig up an accident so any blood in the truck will look like his own."

David's imagination has got us in trouble before, and I know what would happen if Judd catches us snooping around his truck.

"Nope," I say. "Whelan's Garage fixed that truck up for him after the accident. Cleaned the inside and everything. If there was any evidence, it's long gone. Besides, he wouldn't stuff a body in the cab. He'd put it in the back."

David sighs. He don't like to give up a good idea. "Judd could've buried that body down by the creek!" he says.

"Well, the fella from Bens Run must not have been too popular if nobody reported him missing for a month!" I say.

"His family thought he'd gone to visit a cousin in Cincinnati. That's why they didn't report him missing before now," David tells me.

Must be nice, I'm thinking, to have a reporter for a dad—learn all the news before it comes out in the paper.

"There's nothing to say we can't take a look around the bank where Judd's truck went down," David goes on.

"I suppose we can do that," I answer.

Mrs. Howard calls us to lunch then, and this time it's turkey sandwiches with turkey soup. I think I've seen enough turkey to last me awhile, but the real disappointment is there's leftover mince pie for dessert. Just about the time I'm wondering if she invited me to help eat up leftovers, though, David's mom says, "Now if you'd rather have chocolate chunk cookies, Marty, I've got those, too."

"I'd rather have the cookies," says David.

"Me, too," I tell her.

She smiles and takes the pie away and comes back with a plate of homemade cookies and two bowls of mint chocolate-chip ice cream.

Only thing I don't like about being at David's house is I got to watch how I talk. Mrs. Howard don't—doesn't—correct me the way Miss Talbot does at school, but she'll repeat my words using the right ones, and then I know I made a mistake.

"Well, deer hunting season began last Monday," she says as she removes a tea bag from her cup. "At least Judd Travers won't be out there shooting. I suppose your dad will go hunting this weekend?"

"Maybe," I say. "He don't hunt as much as some folks."

"He doesn't?" she says, and I know I got to say it over.

"No, ma'am, he doesn't," I tell her. David grins.

Miss Talbot tells me I'm smart enough to be almost anything I want if I just work on my grammar, so I'm trying.

After lunch we fool around up in David's room. He's got this revolving light, and if you close all the shades and turn it on, it sends sparkles of light, like snowflakes, swirling over the walls and ceiling.

It's time to go home before I'm ready—we're having a really good time—but when Mr. Howard pulls up, David's mom says he's driving me home. David gets his coat and goes along.

"They find out any more about that man from Bens Run?" David asks his dad.

"I haven't heard anything. Only that the cousin in Cincinnati says he never showed up there."

"Is the sheriff investigating?" asks David.

"He's asking around," says his dad.

Just before I get out of the car, David whispers, "Remember! Next time I come over, we check out the creek bank."

Five

Saturday mornings I work for John Collins, the veterinarian down in St. Marys. Dad drops me off early and I change the paper in the pens, scrub the floor, clean the dog run, refill the water and food bowls, and answer the phone. Sometimes, if his assistant's busy, I'll put on the thick gloves Doc Collins keeps around and help get a balky cat out of a cage or something.

I got to know Doc Collins when we took Shiloh in for his shots, and it was him who told me how to get a dog settled down and trusting again after Judd's other three dogs were set loose once. Never did find out who did it, but could have been anyone. Michael Sholt's dad said he might of thought of it himself just to get even with Judd for all he did when he was drinking. Judd sure made a lot of enemies. The talk is that it was the man down in Bens Run who'd had a fight with Judd that did it. Now, of course, the man from Bens Run is missing.

The longer I work for John Collins, the more I want to be a vet. A vet's assistant, anyway. This morning I'm counting sacks of dog and cat food in the supply room so we'll know how much to order.

John Collins is so busy he hardly knows what to tackle first. No sooner get a dog vaccinated or a rabbit patched up than here come a parrot or a snake. The way I see it, a vet has to know a whole lot more than a people doctor, 'cause what's a parrot and a snake got in common? I'd like to know.

Eleven o'clock and John Collins pours himself a cup of coffee.

"Doc Collins," I say, "a few more weeks and Judd Travers is going to get his three dogs back. I was wondering how he could keep them from turning mean again, now that somebody's been kind to 'em."

"Well, just like people, you can't always predict what they'll do," he says. "Some folks who grow up in the worst kind of homes manage to make something of themselves, and others lash out—want to treat everybody the way they were treated. Same with a dog."

"So what should Judd do?"

"For starters, I'd fence my yard so I wouldn't have to chain them up again. You chain a dog, he knows he's not free to fight if he's attacked, so he tries to appear as ferocious as he can. And Judd should certainly stop kicking them around the way he used to, beating on them with a stick. That's just common sense."

Dad picks me up at noon in his Jeep and drives me home along his mail route. Takes about ten times as long to get home this way as if we just drove it straight—Sellers Road, Dancers Lane, Cow House Run Road—but I don't complain. He hands me the mail to put in the boxes, and I turn

28

up the little red flag on the box to let folks know there's something in it, so they don't have to come all the way down their driveway if there's not. Out where we live, the houses are little, but the land is big.

You feel real bad for people who don't get any mail at all. Some folks are tickled just to get a catalog. What I like, though, is finding something in the box for Dad—a piece of pie, maybe. This morning Mrs. Harris leaves a paper plate with five chocolate cupcakes on it. She waves to us from her window up on the hill, and we wave back. I eat my cupcake right away.

"Judd's going to be getting his dogs back soon," I say, wiping my hands on my jeans, and I tell Dad what John Collins says about how chaining a dog makes it mean.

Dad gives a sigh. "Marty, don't you never quit? You're makin' an old man of me, I swear it. You couldn't rest till you got Shiloh for your own, and now you're worrying about those other three dogs."

"But they've settled down some, Dad. Be a shame to chain 'em all over again."

"Maybe so," says Dad, "but I know better than to tell a man how he should be raising his dogs. And I got a whole lot of other things to think on besides that."

I got other things to think about, too, and soon's I get home, I stretch out on the floor, my head on Shiloh, and put my mind to Christmas. He makes the best backrest! I got eighteen dollars saved so far from working for John Collins. Work for Doc Murphy, too, only he takes my pay off the bill I owe him. It was him who stitched up Shiloh after the German shepherd tore him up last summer. At Doc's I'd trim the grass around his fence. He don't mind the mowing, but hates the trimming. With winter coming on, though, he finds other jobs for me to do.

I'm trying to think what to get Dara Lynn. Got the other gifts decided on. Becky's was easy—a tiny yellow bear, the kind you hang on a tree, fluffy as a new mitten, holdin' a box with two Whitman's chocolates in it. Got Ma a cassette tape of her favorite country singer, and for Dad, a giant-sized coffee mug.

Dara Lynn's gift, though, is giving me fits because the pure truth of the matter is I don't want to waste a nickel on her. Far back as I can remember, she's envied every nice thing that ever happened to me and rejoiced in the bad. Like the time I found a dollar bill at the county fair, and she was mad as hornets it wasn't her that saw it first. And then, when I lost it on the Ferris wheel— it blows right out of my hand and goes floating down over the crowd—she almost falls out of the seat laughing.

Nothing makes her smile as wide as when I got to go outside in the cold to do a job I don't like, and she gets to stay indoors eating buttered popcorn. Don't know why the feeling grew up between us like it did, but lately it's been worse than ever.

Dara Lynn's my sister, though, and I got to get her something, so I settle on a cocoa sampler I seen in Sistersville, three different flavors in a little wooden box.

I don't offer up one word about inviting Judd Travers to our house for Christmas, and at dinner that night, I'm glad to hear Ma say that Doc Murphy told her Judd was going off to visit friends at Christmas. Only Doc don't believe him, because as far as anyone knows, Judd don't have hardly any friends. Not the kind to invite you for Christmas, anyway.

"What I think," says Ma, "is that Judd made the story up so nobody would feel sorry for him. One thing he can't stand is people feeling sorry."

I got one hand under the table giving Shiloh a bite of

my chicken, feelin' how glad I am he belongs to me and not to Judd. Do you know how lucky you are, dog? I'm thinkin'. You know how hard I had to work to make you mine? But just when I'm most grateful that Judd won't ruin *this* holiday, I find out it's going to be ruined anyway.

"We're going to have a different kind of Christmas this year," Dad tells us. "Going to drive to Clarksburg on Christmas Day and have dinner with your Aunt Hettie, then go see Grandma Preston in the nursing home."

There is nothing I can say, because I know it's kind and good to go, but there is not one small inch of me that wants to visit a nursing home on Christmas. I don't say a word because I know Dara Lynn will do it for me. She sets up such a howling you'd think she caught her finger in the door.

"Not the whole daaaay!" she wails. "I don't wanna sit in a nursing home with an old woman who goes around stealing false teeth!"

Grandma Preston's got quite a reputation in that nursing home for takin' things from other people's rooms.

"Dara Lynn, your grandma wouldn't do half of what she does if she had her mind back," says Dad. "She might not even know who we are, but it's not fair that Hettie has to spend all her holidays alone with Mother. We're going to do what we can."

"Good-bye, Christmas!" Dara Lynn sings out, and it's a miracle to me she don't get a slap on the mouth.

It snows on Sunday—first big snow of the season. Not some little half-inch job where you can still see sticks and stones underneath, but four or five inches of stuff so white you got to squint your eyes when the sun's on it. Wind blows it high against the shed.

Ma hates to see snow ruined by footprints, but she

31

knows we got to go try it out. She helps Becky on with her boots and jacket, and when we find our caps and mittens, she turns us loose.

We spend the first five minutes just laughing at Shiloh— the way he leaps up over the snow, disappearing down into a snowbank, then makin' another leap and another. He looks like a porpoise. Ma and Dad come out on the porch to watch.

A big clump of snow falls off a tree and lands on Shiloh's head. We throw snowballs at him then, and he tries to catch them in his mouth. He's running and barking and chasing and skidding, and by the time Dad gets out our sled, there are dog-crazy tracks all over the place.

Dara Lynn drags the sled to the top of our hill and I haul up Becky. I settle myself on the sled, Becky between my knees, heels dug deep in the snow. The plan is that Dara Lynn'll give us a push, then jump on behind me, but when I lift my feet and Dara Lynn pushes, she goes down on her knees and the sled takes off without her, Dara Lynn screechin' bloody murder.

I take Becky and the sled back up and this time Dara Lynn gets in the middle and I crawl on behind. We are flying down that hill, coming to a stop between the henhouse and the shed. We've just started back up for a third time when the crack of a rifle sings out, then another. Way up at the top of our hill, we see a buck go leaping across the field.

"Marty!" Dad yells from the doorway. "You kids get in here! Now!"

We leave the sled where it is, and run for the house. We know it's not Judd Travers up there, but even though we got the woods posted, there are always other hunters, other rifles.

"I wish this season was over," says Ma, closing the door behind us.

Six

It stays cold and windy, so David Howard don't come to check out the creek bank like he'd said. We decide we'll wait till after Christmas.

Usually our family cuts our own pine tree to bring inside, but this year—with us driving to Clarksburg and all—Dad says why don't we just string lights on the cedar outside the window? No need to do all that decorating when we won't be here on Christmas Day.

Becky hasn't had enough Decembers yet to care, but Dara Lynn sets up a bellow could've attracted a moose.

"We have to sit outside and open our presents in the snow?" she wails.

But there's new snow come Christmas Eve, and the lights of the tree shine on the ice and make a prettier tree than we ever had inside.

So we just sit at the living room window Christmas morning, eating our pancakes and opening our gifts. Ma loves the cassette I give her, Dad uses my mug for his coffee, Becky eats her Whitman's chocolates, and Dara Lynn even likes the cocoa. I bought a box of doggie treats for Shiloh, and we hide them under all the wrapping paper. He goes nuts trying to trace the smell. Paper and ribbon all over the place. He finds the box and I toss the treats up in the air, one at a time—make him snap at them. Whew! That dog's breath is somethin'!

Ma and Dad give me a new pair of jeans, a Western shirt, and a Pittsburgh Steelers watch.

We change our clothes to go to Aunt Hettie's and, leavin' Shiloh behind, climb in the Jeep. He don't like it one bit when we go off without him; follows the Jeep right down to the road, like any minute we're going to realize we left the most important thing and whistle for him to climb in. When we don't, he trots back up to the house, tail between his legs. I sure do wish dogs could understand English, you could explain things to 'em.

I don't like Shiloh bein' left outside during hunting season, but Ma says it's good to have a dog guarding your house when you're away. Anybody come up our drive with the wrong idea in mind, he might think twice if a barking dog comes out to meet him.

We're only a couple miles down the road when Dara Lynn's got to go to the toilet.

"For heaven's sake," Ma scolds. "If it was Becky, I could understand, but you're almost eight now, Dara Lynn!"

"It's not like I planned it," she shoots back, and we got to stop at Sweeneys' house, ask if we can use their bathroom. Ma takes Becky in, too, for good measure, and I stay in the car with Dad, my faced turned toward Middle Island Creek, embarrassed.

We start off again, Becky's car seat in the middle of the back so's to separate me and Dara Lynn. But she'll stretch her body from one side of the Jeep to the other just to rile me. I'm sitting here minding my own business, and I can feel Dara Lynn's shoe kickin' my leg. She's wriggled down so far that her seat belt's up under her armpits.

"Get on over there where you belong," I say, giving her leg a punch.

Dara Lynn sits up, but this time she spreads her arm across the back of the seat behind Becky so that she's rapping me on the side of my head.

"Stop it, Dara Lynn!" I say, punching her arm, but my elbow bonks Becky, who gives a squeal.

"Marty, keep it down back there. I can't drive and be referee, too," yells Dad. Ma turns and gives us a look.

It's always me gets the blame 'cause I'm the oldest. I wish Dara Lynn could be the oldest for one whole day. I'd get her in so much trouble she'd beg to be let off.

In Clarksburg, Aunt Hettie's waiting at the door, and she don't look anything like Dad, which makes me feel better, 'cause I sure don't want to look like Dara Lynn when I'm grown. Don't want anyone to know we're related. Hettie's wide about the hips, and her arms are round, but she's got Dad's smile, all right. When she hugs you, you know you been hugged.

"You just get on over here and see what's under the tree," she says.

Mostly it's candy, the homemade kind—lollipops for Becky, fudge for me, and peanut brittle for Dara Lynn. Dara Lynn hates peanut brittle, and her mouth turns down so at the corners Ma has to give her a nudge. But Aunt Hettie has dinner waiting with roast beef so juicy I wish Shiloh was there so I could share mine with him.

"Now you've got to be prepared for that nursing home," says Aunt Hettie as we finish her caramel spice cake. "It's not the finest in the world, but the nurses do the best they can."

We go see Grandma right after we eat, before Becky turns cranky, needing her nap. I guess what hits you when you walk in a nursing home—this one, anyway—is that it don't—doesn't—smell so good. Like the bathroom needs cleaning and the food's overcooked. There's eight or ten people in a room with a television in it, all of 'em watching a boys' choir singing "O Holy Night." Two of the women are asleep, and one old lady, tied to her wheelchair with a bed-sheet, is tapping on her tray with a spoon.

We sign in at the desk, and a young woman in a red Santa Claus cap says that Grandma's around somewhere, and then here she comes, flyin' down the hall in her wheel-chair, banging her gums together 'cause she hasn't put her teeth in yet, asking everyone did they see her snow shovel.

Dad goes over and stops the wheelchair before she can run into the artificial tree.

"Merry Christmas, Mother," he says, kissing her cheek. "I brought the family to see you."

"It was right outside my door," says Grandma, not making any sense.

"What was, Mother?" asks Dad.

"My brand-new snow shovel, right outside my door," she says, and fastens her eyes on me. "You take my shovel?"

"No, ma'am," I say.

Becky's backing away, trying to squeeze behind Ma's legs, but Dara Lynn's just staring, her eyes bugging out like a frog's.

"We brought you a present, Grandma," says Ma, putting a box in her lap.

36

Grandma tears away at that wrapping paper, got fingers like claws, almost, nobody to cut her nails except Hettie, and Ma leans down to help get the ribbon off. Grandma pulls out a robe, a rose-colored robe with a flower on each pocket.

"It's got to have pockets," says Grandma, handing it back to her, "I don't want a robe without pockets." Ma tries to show her the pockets, but Grandma's talkin' about somethin' else now. It pains Ma, I can tell.

The nurse comes over and suggests we wheel Grandma around the nursing home so she can see the decorations in the dining room and parlor. It gives us something to do. Ma and Aunt Hettie stay in the reception room to talk, but Dad pushes Grandma's wheelchair, and us kids troop along.

Becky's got the idea that we come to see Santa, and now she spots some old man with a beard sitting at his window.

"There's Santa!" she yells excitedly. The man turns and laughs.

"Come here, sweetheart," he says, holding out his arms, and I take Becky inside his room to say hello. She sits on his lap and tells him what all she got for Christmas, and he's so tickled. Becky don't even notice he only has one leg.

But Grandma wants to go. "That man is *no good!*" she says to Dara Lynn. "He stole my change purse."

"Mother, your change purse is right there in your pocket," Dad tells her as we start off again, and Becky waves to the man with the beard.

But Grandma goes on about how she lives in a den of thieves and liars, and how if Dad really loved her, he'd get her out of this place.

It hurts Dad, 'cause it was more than Aunt Hettie could

37

manage to care for Grandma at home, and it'd be even worse for Ma, with a family to look after, too.

"I ever get old and crazy, just shoot me," murmurs Dara Lynn.

After we tour the whole building and take Grandma back to her room, we read the Bible together and then we all sing "Silent Night." For the first time, Grandma gets real quiet—studies us hard while we're singin'—and I see tears in her eyes, like maybe for the first time she remembers who we are.

But by the time we get our coats, she wants to roam around in her wheelchair again. She's got her new robe over her shoulders like a cape now, won't let nobody touch it, and says she's got to go see the man with the beard and get her change purse back.

The attendant winks at us. "You go on," she says. "I'll handle this."

So we go back out to the Jeep, and spend the rest of the day at Aunt Hettie's. Becky takes a nap on her bed, and Dara Lynn and me put together a jigsaw puzzle of a pepperoni pizza, and I'm thinking how Dara Lynn and me are getting along fine right now, why can't we get along like this all the time? I wonder does it have anything to do with Shiloh being my dog, when all the while what Dara Lynn really wanted was a kitten?

We have a light supper before we leave—cold roast beef sandwiches—and then we set out. Sky's almost dark, but the snow gives off light so it don't seem as late as it is. Starts to snow some more, too.

Ma says, "It's always hard to visit Grandma and it's always hard to leave." Her own ma died a few years back, so Dad's is the only ma she's got.

We see we left the lights shining on our outdoor Christmas tree when we pull in the drive, and it's a welcome sight, but I'm lookin' around for Shiloh. Usually he'd be dancin' down the drive by now, head goin' one way, tail the other.

"Where's Shiloh?" Becky asks, missing him, too.

"Probably running around with that black Labrador, I'll bet," says Ma. "Nice that he's got a friend."

I'm thinking, though, that it's not often our whole family's gone the way we were today. Usually Ma's home while Dad's at work and we're in school. But this time we've been gone from almost eleven in the morning to eight at night, time enough for a dog to wonder if you're ever comin' back. Go lookin' for you, maybe.

We walk inside and turn on the TV to get the last of the Christmas music we'll hear all year, and when my Steelers watch says ten o'clock and Shiloh's still not back, I put on my boots and jacket and go out on the porch.

First I just stand on the steps and whistle. Never did learn to whistle like Dad can, though. Mine's a puny little noise that don't travel much beyond the cedar tree.

"Shiloh!" I call, and my voice echoes against the hills. "Here, boy! Shiloh! Come on, boy!"

Nothin' stirs but the bushes, branches blowin'.

I clump down to the end of the drive, hands in my pockets, shoulders hunched.

"Shiloh!" I yell, loud as my lungs will let me. "Shi . . . loh! Shi . . . loh!" Air's so still I figure that dog should be able to hear me a half mile off.

Then I stand real still and listen. Used to be I could hear his feet scurrying through the field or down the path from the meadow, but I know that with all the snow, that dog could be right behind me and I wouldn't hear a thing 'cept his collar jingling.

I walk to the bridge and yell some more, then go left and follow the road in the other direction, bellowing like a new calf.

Nothin' answers but the wind.

Seven

It's hard to sleep that night. Our sofa's got more lumps than bean soup, and every time I turn over, I pull out the blanket from the bottom.

I get up about two in the morning and stand at the window. Moon's almost full, and the snow sparkles like diamonds. I'm not lookin' for moonlight or snowlight, though—only Shiloh. We keep the shed door open on nights like this so he can go in there and sleep if he comes back late. But I know my dog; he'd make at least one detour up on the porch first to see if somebody was awake to let him in. Not a fresh paw print anywhere.

I'm thinking of the hunters we heard up in our woods. Deer season's over now, but there's possum and coon to hunt; rabbit and groundhog, too. What if a hunter took it in his head to steal Shiloh? You ride along and see notices posted on trees about a dog missing, and most of the time someone's made off with it—someone who wants a good hunting dog, or a watchdog, or both.

I get this sick feeling—what if I never see Shiloh again? What if somebody's got him chained, beatin' on him like Judd used to do? All I got to remember him by are yesterday's paw prints, most of 'em half covered now by new snow. I lay back down and fall asleep out of sheer sadness.

Don't have to go to school till the second of January, so Ma lets us sleep in next day. Can't believe I sleep till nine thirty, and I only wake then because I hear dogs yipping out in the yard. I sit straight up.

"Shiloh's back!" says Ma from the kitchen. "My stars, what's that dog got now?"

I leap off the couch and run to the door. There's Shiloh and the black Lab. Shiloh's got a piece of orange rag in his mouth, and they're playin' and tuggin' at it. Thing about dogs, they can get enjoyment out of the most common ordinary object you could ever imagine. I'm so happy to see him I pull on my jeans, push my feet in my shoes, and grab my jacket. I run outside and wade through the snow to where Shiloh and the Labrador are chasing each other around and barking.

Rag looks like a piece of vest a traffic cop wears. I'm hoping those dogs didn't get in somebody's clothes basket or, worse yet, run off with somethin' belonging to the sheriff. I stick the rag in my jacket pocket and reach down to hug my dog. "You're weird," I tell him. "You and your friend both." He gives me the wettest kiss this side the Mississippi.

When I go in the house, Shiloh follows for his breakfast,

42

and the Labrador trots off, lookin' for some other mischief. Becky's up, wantin' me to play Candy Land with her—most boring game in the whole world, but I do.

Ma's feeling good this morning, I can tell. Shiloh's back, Christmas is over, she's done her duty by Grandma Preston, and she's in the kitchen making cinnamon rolls. She sings along with the cassette I give her:

> "The roughest road in the valley,
> Longest I ever did roam,
> But the sweetest path in the country,
> Because it leads me home."

I tell Dara Lynn it's her turn to play Candy Land with Becky, and I call up David Howard. After I hear what he got for Christmas, my presents don't sound all that much. He got two computer games, a pair of Nike Air Gridstar crosstrainers, a basketball, a sleeping bag, four books, a Chicago Bulls T-shirt, and a horn for his bike. And that was just from his folks. He still has presents coming from his grandparents.

"Why don't I come over to your house tomorrow, and we'll check out the creek bank where Judd had his accident?" says David.

"Okay with me," I tell him.

Dad's got the *Tyler Star–News* with him when he comes home, and while he sits in the kitchen talking to Ma, I take the paper in on the sofa and look through it, see if there's anything more about the missing man from Bens Run. Don't find anything of interest except a story about a car crash up in Wheeling, an escape from the county jail, a robbery up in Sistersville, and a hunter who shot a man over in

43

Marion County by mistake. Nothing about nobody from Bens Run.

David Howard's mom drives him over the next morning, and it's the kind of gray winter day that can't decide if it's going to rain or snow. We plan to head out for Middle Island Creek soon as we eat lunch. Becky, of course, goes and asks David to play Candy Land with her, but he don't have little sisters, and don't know you got to let Becky win. When it's him doing the winning, Becky slides down off the chair and runs in the bedroom, then comes back out later with a towel over her head so no one can see she's been cryin'. David must think I got the strangest family!

Ma says lunch is ready. It's only hot dogs and soup, but there's cinnamon rolls for dessert, the frosting still warm.

"You boys playing in or out this afternoon?" Ma asks.

"Out," I tell her. "Maybe do some hiking."

We put on our jackets and head down to the bridge, Shiloh trotting along behind. I point out the place the pickup went over, and we crawl down the bank, our feet turned sideways.

"Nothing to see!" I say to David. "Everything's covered with snow."

But David keeps going. The thing about David Howard is he don't let real life get in the way of his imagination. If he wants to find clues that Judd Travers murdered the man from Bens Run, then David'll find plenty; just won't happen to be the right clues, that's all.

Shiloh's comin' down the hill after us, glad to be doin' whatever we are, though he's no idea in the world what that is.

David turns and points at Shiloh. "Sniff!" he says.

Shiloh wags his tail.

"What you doing, David?"

"I'm telling him to sniff. If there was a dead body buried down here, I'll bet a dog could find it."

I laugh. "Shiloh don't even know the word 'sniff,' " I tell him. So David says it again, and gets down on all fours, trying to show my dog what to do. I fall down in the snow laughing my head off, and Shiloh falls on top of me, joinin' in the fun.

We're rolling around on the bank, havin' a wrestling match, when all of a sudden my knee hits somethin' hard.

"Ow!" I yell, and push David off me.

Shiloh comes runnin' over like a snowplow, pushin' up snow with his nose, and before you can blink, he's dug up a man's boot, frozen hard as cement.

Eight

David and I sit on our knees in the snow, turning that boot over and over.

"Evidence!" says David, his eyes snappin'. "This could put Judd Travers behind bars for life."

That's the way folks feel about Judd, see. They remember how he was—and maybe still is, far as I know. His meanness to dogs and people, the way he cheated and lied. When you've done all the things Judd did, how do you get folks to start trusting you? It's true he might be tryin' to change, but the tryin' part still needed a lot of work.

"David, you don't even know whose boot that is!" I say. David Howard's case against Judd is as stupid as flypaper in winter. "Even if it *does* belong to that man from Bens Run, and even if Judd *did* murder him, just 'cause he wrecked his truck here don't mean that's where the man is buried. The one don't have a single thing to do with the other."

Even Shiloh's laughin'. Sittin' there in the snow with his mouth open. Sure looks like a grin to me.

But David says, "You know how a criminal always returns to the scene of the crime? He just can't help himself! Same with Judd Travers. Maybe his conscience drove him here."

If I was a teacher and this was homework, I'd give David a failing grade. One thing sure, he's never going to let himself be bored, and that's what I like about David Howard: He don't have enough excitement, he'll make it up.

We walk upcreek for a spell, watching a flock of ducks fly low over the water. Probably going to light down on one of the islands out in the middle. A little farther on, we can make out Judd's trailer across Middle Island Creek.

"Who named this a creek instead of a river? Paul Bunyan?" says David. "Sure looks like a river to me."

"We walk far enough, we'd get up to Michael Sholt's cousin's house," I tell him. Michael lives down toward Friendly, but his cousin lives way upcreek and takes a different bus to school.

"If we walk far enough we'll get to the North Pole!" says David. Think he's getting a little tired of all this hiking. Getting cold, leastways. Probably got his mind on Ma's cinnamon rolls.

"Want to go back?" I ask.

"Yeah," he says. "But keep the boot."

I don't know what I'm going to do with a frozen shoe, but I throw it under the porch steps when we get home, and we eat a plate of cinnamon rolls.

On Sunday, Ma's listening to Brother Jonas preach on TV and Dad's cleaning his razor. Dara Lynn and Becky have pulled bedsheets over a couple chairs in their room to make a tent, and they're pretending that Shiloh's a bear, tryin' to get in. The more they squeal, the more Shiloh wiggles about, tryin' to get his nose under the edge of the sheet, tail going ninety miles an hour. If that dog had wings, he'd fly, except his propeller would be on the wrong end.

"I'm going over to visit Judd—see how he's doing," I tell Dad.

Dad don't look at me, just frowns a little at his razor. "You could always pick up the phone," he says, not too sure, I guess, about me goin' over alone to visit a man like Judd, no matter how many chances he'd give him.

"I might could give him a hand with somethin', help him out," I say.

"Well, don't stay too long," says Dad.

Outside, I pull that boot out from under the steps, tuck it under my arm, and start off.

I cross the bridge, Shiloh beside me, and watch to see if he'll come ahead or turn back. This time he goes a few steps beyond the other side, then sits down in the snow and whimpers. I walk on about fifty yards and look back over my shoulder. Shiloh's trottin' back across the bridge. Guess he's decided not to freeze his bottom waiting for me.

Sky is bright, but cold. Sun don't seem to warm me at all. The thing about West Virginia is it takes so long for the sun to come up over those hills on one side of the creek that it don't seem any time at all before it's sliding down behind the hills on the other. Boy, you live in Kansas, flat as an ironing board, I'll bet the sun comes up in the morning before you even open your eyes. You go to bed, it's still got a way to go before it's down.

Then I realize I'm not cold from the weather, I'm cold

48

from fear. The goose bumps I can feel popping out on my arms under my jacket don't have nothing to do with the snow. Shiloh had the right idea turning back. What I am fixing to do is walk right up to Judd Travers holding the one piece of evidence he just might kill for to get. Could be he's thinkin' on digging around over on that bank himself as soon as his leg gets better, and here I am, showing him what I got, what David and me know.

I got this far, though, I got to go on. If Judd's looking out of his trailer now, he's already seen me comin', knows what I got. I wonder if there's a rifle pointed at me right this very minute.

Climb the steps to his trailer and knock, but I don't hear any sound at all from inside—no TV, no radio. Can hear my teeth chattering. I hug my arms tight around my body, the boot still tucked under my arm, and knock again. Then I hear this engine. I turn around, and here come Judd's pickup. He gets out, hauling his left leg down first, then his crutches. The cast is a dirty white, but nobody's wrote his name on it or anything, the way they'd do at school. He don't have his gun with him, and that cheers me right quick.

"Hey!" I call. "You're driving now!"

"I can get where I want to go, that's about it," Judd says. He unfolds himself like an old man. Got a paper sack in his hand, and I hope it's not whiskey.

I knew that as soon as Judd could start driving again, he would, because he loves his truck almost more than anything else in this world. Washes it every weekend, and finds any excuse he can to drive to Friendly and back, just ridin' around, listenin' to his radio. Last summer, on the Saturdays he wasn't working, wouldn't be anything at all to see Judd passing three or four times out on the road, goin' nowhere in particular.

He's comin' slow up his board walk, cast and crutches tapping a rhythm like old Peg Leg the Pirate. "What you doin' over this way?" he wants to know.

"Just came to say hello, see how you're doin'."

"Well, I'm alive," he tells me.

Judd goes in first, leaves the door open behind him, and I figure that's all the invitation I'm gonna get, so I go in, too. Close the door. I guess what I plan to do is show him the boot and ask does he know who it belongs to. I figure I can tell by the look on his face if it belongs to that man from Bens Run, and if Judd's the reason he disappeared. With Judd hobbling about on that leg of his, I can be out the door and in the bushes if he gets mad.

Judd puts the sack on his table, then reaches inside and pulls out a half gallon of milk, some bread, and a tin of sardines.

"What you got there?" Judd asks, nodding toward the boot.

I swallow. "Oh, just somethin' I wonder if you'd recognize," I say, and hold it up. Wonder if I'm sounding smart-mouth.

Judd's jaw drops and he stares at it for a moment. "Where'd you find it?"

"Over by the creek." I study his face, my heart thumpin' hard. "Know who it belongs to?"

"Of course," says Judd. "It's mine."

Talk about feelin' stupid! I don't tell him what David Howard figured.

"Never thought I'd see *that* again! Couldn't wear it anyway, it's soaked up so much rain and snow. Most of my clothes, they just cut them off, you know. In the emergency room, they don't fool around." He takes the boot and throws it back into his bedroom.

"Didn't you miss it when you dressed to come home from the hospital?"

"Missed it before then, so a guy from work brought me a pair of his old sneakers to get home in. You want a pop or somethin'?" Judd asks me.

"Okay." I sit down on Judd's couch, remembering how only a few months past, he had me workin' out there in the summer sun in order to earn his dog, and then, when I'm about done, tells me I can't have Shiloh after all—that nobody witnessed our agreement, and I'm a fool to do all that work. Guess I'd have to say it was the worst day of my life. No—the worst hadn't happened yet; I'm gettin' to that—but it was a time I'll never forget.

Judd gets me a 7Up from his refrigerator and pours himself a mug of leftover coffee. Then he sits down, his jacket still on, 'cause he keeps his trailer cold. Holds the cup under his chin, lettin' the steam warm his face.

"So how's things?" he asks.

"Okay," I tell him. "I been working for that vet down in St. Marys on Saturday mornings. Learnin' a lot about dogs."

"Yeah?" says Judd.

"We see a lot of dogs that have been chained up, and most of 'em are mean as nails. John Collins—he's the vet—says it's because they feel trapped that way. If something came along to attack 'em, they'd be in a tough spot 'cause they can't fight free, so they act real fierce to scare you off."

"That a fact?" says Judd, and I'm tryin' to read his face as he takes another drink of coffee. "Well," he says at last, "I

51

sure know how it is to feel cornered. Know what it's like to feel trapped."

I don't say nothing. I'm remembering what Doc Murphy told me about how he knew the Traverses when Judd was a little kid, and how the father used to whip those kids with the buckle end of a belt.

Judd stares out the window beyond my head like he don't hardly see me at all. And suddenly he stands up and says, "Well, I'm goin' to take a nap, Marty." That's a good-bye if I ever heard one, so I set my empty pop can on the floor.

"Okay," I say. "See you around."

I'm halfway across his yard when I realize what I've done. My hands feel all clammy. Why do I think I can believe Judd Travers? If David Howard *was* right, and Judd done something to that man from Bens Run, and if that boot belonged to him, you can bet Judd'll burn it faster than a dog can pee. Why didn't I ask to see that other boot—see if it matched? I can't believe how stupid I am—just handed the evidence right over!

Figure I got to steal a look in the back of his pickup as I walk by, see if there're any clues in there. Judd keeps all sorts of stuff in there, but he's got a tarp over it now, and the tarp's covered with snow. I manage to lift a corner and peer underneath. Piece of plywood, a coil of rope, truck battery, tires, roofing shingles, iron pipe, canvas. . . .

And then I see Judd Travers watchin' me from his window. I drop that tarp right quick, give him a wave, and head on home. Feel like the worst kind of fool.

But I feel even worse later. Walk in the house and Ma says, "David called, Marty. Wants you to call him back right away."

I go out in the kitchen and dial David's number.

"Marty!" he says. "Guess what?"

I kid around. "They found the guy from Bens Run with a bullet in his head?"

There's silence from the other end. Then, "There wasn't any bullet, but they found him. And he's dead."

Nine

I don't see David again till we go back to school after New Year's. By then I'm ready for vacation to be over. Becky's come down with chicken pox, and Dara Lynn's stepped on my Steelers watch and broke the glass. Now we got to send it all the way to the factory for a new face cover, which means I can't wear it on the first day back to school.

Big news is that the man from Bens Run died of a blow to the head, says the *Tyler Star–News*, and David and I been on the phone to each other most every day about it. Body was found down along the Ohio River by a highway maintenance crew, but the man's shoes were missing. Murder weapon's missing, too, and David's sure Judd's the one who done it. I'm not so sure about the shoes—they could have come off and floated most anywhere. I'm thinking about the murder weapon. What I'm remembering, and wish I wasn't, is that piece of iron pipe in the back of Judd's pickup.

School bus comes up our road as far as the bridge, then turns around. Anybody living on the other side has to walk over here or catch another bus somewhere else. I think it's because that old bridge might not hold a bus full of kids. Fire truck come up once makin' a safety run, and had to empty its tank before it crossed, then fill up again from the other side of the creek.

Driver picks up anybody who's ready on the way up, and everybody else on the way back, so that kids who live along this route got two chances to catch the bus.

"Happy New Year, Marty," says Mrs. Sims, the driver. "How you doin', Dara Lynn?"

Dara Lynn never smiles at nobody before nine o'clock in the morning, and she don't say nothing, but I wish Mrs. Sims a Happy New Year, too, and go sit across from Michael Sholt. Out the window I can see Shiloh trotting back up the lane to the house. Ma says that sometimes after we're gone in the mornings, she picks that dog up and rocks him like a baby. Don't many dogs have a grown woman who'll do that, I'll bet.

"Heard the news?" Michael crows as soon as I step on the bus. "The man from Bens Run was found murdered, and they think Judd did it."

"*Who* thinks?" I say.

"*Everybody!*" says Fred Niles. "Everyone's talking that it's Judd!"

Sarah Peters is up on her knees on the seat so she can see around the whole bus. "The sheriff's questioning a whole lot of people, and one of 'em's Judd. It was on the news this morning." I see pretty quick that whether Judd done it or not, the feelin's going against him.

"Just because they questioned him don't mean he did it," I say.

"How come you're stickin' up for Judd, Marty?" asks Sarah. "Thought you used to hate him worse'n poison."

"Maybe he's tryin' to change. You ever think of that?" I ask her. But I don't even know that myself.

One by one, other kids climb on, and everyone's wearin' a little something they got for Christmas—a jacket or sneakers or cap. By the time David gets on, the other kids are looking at Michael Sholt's baseball cards and telling what all they got for Christmas. David sits down beside me.

"Anything new?" I ask.

"Judd was called in for questioning, but the sheriff released him," David says. "Doesn't mean he's innocent. It just means they haven't charged him with anything yet."

"Do they know where he was when the guy was murdered?" I ask.

"They don't even know the exact day. It was about the time of Judd's accident, but it could have been a week before or a week after." He looks at me. "I think we better turn that boot over to the sheriff."

I swallow. "I don't have it," I say.

"Where *is* it?"

I'm so miserable, my stomach hurts. "Judd said it was his, so I gave it to him."

David slides down in the seat, can hardly believe it. "We could've been on the witness stand, Marty!" he says. "Maybe we could have solved the case!"

"Just be quiet about it," I say. I'm feeling low enough as it is.

David don't tell the other kids what I did, but he is sure disgusted.

At school, Miss Talbot's wearin' something new she got for Christmas, too. It's a diamond ring, and all the girls got to gather round her desk and make her turn her hand this way and that, see the diamond sparkle. She's engaged to a high school teacher over in Middlebourne.

Soon as the kids start talking about Judd Travers being guilty, though, she puts a stop to it. "This class is not a courtroom," she says, and we know that—ring or no ring—she means business.

At home, Dad won't let us talk about Judd being the murderer, either.

"That Ed Sholt!" he says. "Shootin' off his mouth . . . !" Dad kicks off his shoes and sinks down on the sofa. "Saw him at lunch today in Sistersville, and he's worked out the whole thing in his head—all the different ways the man could have been killed, and he's got Judd doing the killing in every one of 'em. 'Pipe down, Ed,' I tell him. 'A man's innocent till proven guilty, you know. He's a right to his day in court, it ever gets to that.' But he says, 'You're the one who should worry, Ray. You live closer to Judd than the rest of us. If it were me, I'd get a good strong lock for my door and keep a gun handy.'"

I swallow. "You talk to the sheriff yet?"

"Yes, and he's guessing Judd's not the one. They can't tell when the man was killed exactly, not when a body's been dead this long, but they figure he probably died sometime after Judd's accident; somebody thinks he may have seen him later than that, anyway."

I'm wondering what it's like to have everybody suspecting you of a crime you didn't do—just when you're tryin' to be better. Maybe you think, what's the use? If everybody figures you're bad, might as well go ahead and be bad. But if Judd gives up now, those dogs of his, when he gets 'em back, are going to have a worse time of it than before.

Judd'll hate everything and everybody, includin' his dogs. On the other hand, what if he *did* do it? What if he really is a killer?

I try not to let myself think on that. The only thing I can see to do—for Judd's dogs, anyway—is to get Judd Travers a fence. Once I do something for *all* Judd's dogs, I can stop feelin' so guilty about saving only the one. So I say to Dad, "You know anybody got some old chicken wire stuck away that we could use to fence in Judd's yard for his dogs?"

Dad turns the TV down and looks at me. "*Chicken* wire? You got to have somethin' stronger than that, Marty! You need regular fencing wire and metal posts, and nobody I know has a whole fence just sittin' around, I can tell you."

Seem like everything I think of to do has got a hitch to it.

All week the weather stays mild, and the snow's disappearin' fast. "January thaw," Ma says. Tells us that for a few days most Januarys, it seems, there's a mild spell to give us a promise of spring before the next big snowfall.

The sun shines on into the weekend, and Saturday afternoon, after I get back from the vet, I decide that I'm going about this fence idea all wrong. If nobody's going to keep an old fence around after they take it down, then I got to find somebody with the fence still up that he'd just as soon wasn't there.

I walk over to Doc Murphy's, Shiloh frisking alongside me, tryin' to get me to run. I'm thinking how last September, when I was helpin' Doc in his yard, he'd said now that his wife wasn't there to garden anymore, he wished he didn't have a fence around that vegetable plot, just a nuisance when he mowed.

Doc's got a couple of men patching his roof and cleaning

his gutters, and he's out there scattering grass seed on all the bare patches of lawn. Shiloh goes right over and waits for Doc to pet him. I wonder if in his little dog brain he remembers that Doc saved his life after the fight with the German shepherd.

"Hello there, Marty," he says, scratchin' Shiloh behind the ears. "I'm getting a jump on old man winter. Figure if I can get this seed in the ground before the next snow, it'll be the first grass up come spring."

"Too bad that fence is still there, or you could plant right over the postholes," I tell him.

"I was thinking the same thing," says Doc. He lets Shiloh go, and scoops up another handful of seed from his bag.

"I could maybe take it down for you," I offer.

He gives this little laugh. "That's not a job for a kid. Lot of wire there, and those posts are heavy."

"I bet I could. Would haul it away for you, too."

Doc studies me over the rim of his glasses. "Your dad wants this fence?"

"It's for Judd Travers. To keep his dogs happy when he gets 'em back. He won't let 'em run loose, 'cause they're his hunting dogs, but John Collins says they wouldn't be half as mean if they weren't chained—if they had a yard to play in."

Doc Murphy don't say anything for a minute. Just turns his back on me and goes on scattering that seed. Finally he says, "Tell you what: I'll have Joe and Earl there" —and he nods toward the men on the roof— "take that fence down if you can have it off my property by tomorrow. I don't want a pile of fencing sitting around here. Then I can get the whole place seeded in this warm spell. Deal?"

"Deal," I say. "Dad and me'll come pick it up in the morning."

I don't even have time to be happy, because I realize Judd Travers don't know a single solitary thing about any of this. You don't just show up at a man's house and start fencing his yard.

Only thing I can think of to do is walk on over to Judd's and ask. I'm not real eager to go over there by myself, though. I mean, what if that boot we found *did* belong to the dead man, and Judd knows that I know what it looked like? Where it was found? 'Course, why would Judd kill a man, leave his body by the river, but bury his boots someplace else? That don't make a whole lot of sense, either.

I walk back up the road and my mind's goin' around and around, first how Judd must have done it for sure and then how he didn't, like to drive me crazy. I cross the bridge, but when I head for the brown-and-white trailer, Shiloh turns back. I get to Judd's about the time he's sittin' down to lunch.

Any other man would ask me to come back later or invite me to share his food. Judd Travers invites me in to watch him eat, I guess, 'cause I sit at his table and he only offers me a pop. And right off he says:

"What you want? Everybody else seems to think I killed a man. That what you come to say?"

"No," I tell him. "'Course not." Already my heart's knockin' around beneath my jacket.

"Then what were you doin' snoopin' in the back of my truck last time you were here?"

My breath seems to freeze right up inside my chest. One thing about Judd Travers, he don't forget. I decide to tell it straight. "Trying to figure where that other boot of yours was," I tell him. "To match the one I found."

"Why should you care?" asks Judd, his narrow eyes on me.

I shrug. "No particular reason. Just wondering, that's all."

"Well, I threw it out," Judd says. "When you think you've seen the last of one, not much use for the other."

Wonder just how far Judd trusts me; about as far as I trust him, I guess. I talk about somethin' else: "When do you suppose you'll get your dogs back?"

"Soon's I can get around without this cast," he says. "Doc's taking it off next Wednesday. I'll still be hobblin' around on crutches, but I figure I can at least tend to my dogs."

"You know," I say, "the way I hear it, the happiest dogs make the best hunters."

"Don't know about that," says Judd. "My pa always said to keep 'em lean and mean."

Can't help myself. "Maybe your pa wasn't always right," I say.

Judd pauses, a piece of macaroni on his fork. He looks at me for a minute, then puts the fork to his mouth, don't say nothing. I figure that don't get me no points.

"All I know is what I learn from Doc Collins, that chainin' up dogs is one of the worst things you can do," I say.

"Well, that's just a pity, because I don't have no money for a fence," Judd tells me, and takes a big swallow of water, wipes his hand across his mouth, and hunches over his plate again, like his macaroni and beef is a chore he's got to wade through.

"What I come to tell you is that Doc Murphy's having his garden fence took down this afternoon, wants if off his property by tomorrow. First come, first get. I asked him not to give it to nobody till I'd talked to you." I pray Jesus this isn't a true lie, just a social conversation.

61

"What's the catch?" asks Judd.

"Nothin'. He wants to plant grass seed over the post-holes during this warm spell."

"Well, I got the strength of a ninety-year-old man right now, and Doc knows that. I can't be fooling with a fence."

"Dad and me can bring it by. Put it up for you."

Judd gives this half smile and a "*Huh!* Nobody does nothing for free," he says.

"We're not askin' anything, Judd! Just see a chance to do a little something for those dogs."

"Why? They're not your dogs. You got Shiloh. You got an eye on them, too?"

"No! What you talkin' about? We're just bein' neigh-borly, that's all."

"Well, my dogs'll get along fine without you," says Judd, and goes on eating, and my stomach does a flip-flop.

I stand up. "If you don't want it, I know folks who do. What's the name of that man with all those hunting dogs over in Little—those really *fine* dogs? He knows they need a place to run, and he'd like that fence, I'll bet." I am stretch-ing the truth so far I can almost hear it snap. Don't even know a man in Little.

I wait for two . . . three seconds, but Judd don't say a thing. I push my chair in and head out the door.

Ten

All the way home I am chewin' myself out. What am I, some kind of fool? Judd Travers don't care about his dogs any more than I care about mushrooms. Couldn't get that man to change if you was to hold his feet to the fire.

And now I feel a rage buildin' up in my chest that's almost too much for me to handle. All I am trying in this world to do is make life a little easier for Judd Travers's dogs, and what do I get? Trouble up one side and down the other. Bet he *did* kill that man from Bens Run. Judd's got enough meanness in him to do most anything.

Right this very minute Doc's got those men takin' down his fence. I cross the bridge and can look way down the road, see where one is digging up those posts, and the other is winding up that wire. And tomorrow morning my dad, who don't even know it yet, is to drive his Jeep over and pick up a whole yard of fence that Judd Travers don't want in the first place.

I am too mad to go inside our house. Too mad to look myself in the mirror. Shiloh comes out to meet me and I don't even say hello. Just march on by and head up the path to the far hill, Shiloh running on ahead, bouncing with pure joy.

"It's all because of you," I tell him, knowing all the while I'd do it again, even so. It's true, though. If it weren't for Shiloh, Judd Travers would be just somebody to stay away from when we could, say your howdys to when you couldn't. But because I got Shiloh, I am smack in the middle of all Judd's problems.

I'm remembering it was up here I saw that gray fox last summer with the reddish head. Suppose somebody's shot it by now, with all the meanness around. Every minute of every day there are folks like Judd Travers bein' born; every minute of every day they are thinkin' up ways to be worse than they were the day before.

What do I care what happens to Judd? I ask myself. What do I care what happens to his dogs? I am turnin' myself inside out to be nice to a man who hasn't an ounce of kindness in his whole body, and who's probably a killer, too.

All afternoon I stomp and storm around our woods and meadow, pickin' up every limb I can find and whackin' it so hard against a stump I send splinters every which way. Every log becomes a Judd Travers I got to kick and whack, till my feet and arms are tired.

Finally, when I been gone so long I know Ma will worry, when even Shiloh's laid down to rest himself, I turn around and start back. I get home about the time Dad's coming up the drive in his Jeep.

"You look like you been hiking some," Dad says as I follow him into the house where Dara Lynn and Becky are watching TV.

"*Wondered* where you were, Marty," Ma calls from the kitchen.

I throw my jacket on the floor. "I don't want to have anything more to do with Judd Travers the whole rest of my life!" I say.

Now Dad's lookin' at me. "Marty, I don't think I want you going over there alone," he says. "Didn't have a fight with him, did you?"

"No, I didn't have no fight!" I say, a little too loud, and grab a box of cheese crackers from the cupboard like they was out to get me. Lean against the counter and stuff 'em in my mouth, hardly even tasting. I think again how that fence is waiting over there at Doc Murphy's, and figure I'm not just mad, I'm crazy. Whatever Grandma Preston's got wrong with her mind, I got it, too.

But Dad's been delivering the JCPenney spring catalog, and he's too tired to take on my worries. "You'd think it was Christmas all over again, the way folks were waiting for 'em," he says. And then, "Ooof," as he sits down at the table and pulls off his boots. "I don't ever want to get up again. Think I'll spend the night right here in this chair."

Ma laughs and rubs his shoulders.

"I am going to stretch out on that couch and not move except to eat," he tells her.

Telephone rings, and I answer.

It's Judd.

"What kind of fence did you say it was?" he asks.

I blink. Swallow. "Green yard fencing, the wire kind," I tell him, and swallow again. The cheese crackers are dry in my mouth.

65

"Well, I don't want no gate. Don't want anybody sneakin' in, lettin' my dogs loose again."

I stare at the clock above the sink. "What time you want us to come over tomorrow?" I ask.

"Not before nine, that's for sure."

"See you tomorrow, then," I say, and hang up.

I am suddenly so quiet my hand freezes there in the box of crackers. Dad is telling Ma about the deliveries he made that day, and I slip the crackers back on the shelf. Go stare out the window. Now how in the world am I going to tell my dad I volunteered him to put up fencing at Judd's?

"Ground's softening up," I say finally. "Good time to work in the yard."

Dad gives me a sideways glance. "You want to work in the yard, Marty, you got my blessing." He reaches for the mug of coffee Ma pours for him, warm him up a little.

I try again. "Dad, what if you was to find that tomorrow's your one good day to do a really fine deed for a person? And what if I said I'd help out?"

Dad slowly slides that coffee mug back on the table, turns to me, and says, "What in the world have you done now?"

I tell him about Doc Murphy's fence, and what a good thing this would be for Judd's dogs.

"Marty, just two seconds ago you even mention Judd's name, you're spittin' nails!" Ma says.

"Well, a person's got a right to change, hasn't he?" I plead, lookin' at Dad. "Didn't you say you believe in second chances?"

Dad gives such a long, drawn-out sigh you'd think there couldn't be that much air in a human lung.

"We'll see how I feel tomorrow," he says.

Tired as I am, I don't sleep so good. What if Judd changes his mind? What if we haul all those posts over to Judd's tomorrow and, out of sheer spite and meanness, he says to get 'em off his property, he don't want 'em there? Worse yet, what if after all this work, Judd *does* turn out to be the one who murdered the man from Bens Run, and I'm doin' all this work to please the devil?

Next day Dad says he feels better. Not good, but better. The sun helps, so he wants to start early, get it over with, and we drive to Doc's to load that fencing in the Jeep, then make trips back and forth to Judd's till it's all there. I know there's a hundred other things my dad would rather be doing, but when he's got a chance to do what's right or to do what's easy, he can work the legs off most any man in Tyler County.

Judd comes outside, and if he's not exactly friendly, he's helpful. But I never knew that putting up a fence could take so long or be so hard. First thing we do is measure to see just how much of it we can use, bringing it right up to Judd's trailer so's he can step out his back door and into the dog run. Then we lay those posts where they're going to go, and Dad and I take turns with the shovel, digging the holes and packing the dirt in around the posts till they're rock solid. Judd can't do any digging, but he helps uncoil the fencing and fasten it in place. We put the extra behind his shed.

It's well into afternoon before the job's done, and when Dad and me get home, we both stretch out on the living room rug and don't wake up till dinner.

"Judd was about as pleasant today as I've seen him," Dad says to Ma, helpin' himself to the black-eyed peas and ham.

"Maybe so, but I'm still uneasy about him," she answers.

I'm thinking that the sheriff's guess is right. Judd may

have had a fight once with the man from Bens Run, but he probably wasn't the one who killed him. 'Course, they could have had a second fight, and Judd killed him not meaning to. That's another way it could have happened.

That don't keep me from going over to Judd's on Wednesday after school to see the neighbor on one side of Judd bring the two dogs he's been keepin', and the folks on the other side bring over the one. Those dogs don't know which to smell first, the new fence or each other. They get to yippin' and runnin' around in wider and wider circles like they can't believe their freedom. We laugh at their craziness. I reach out every time a dog comes by, like I'm tryin' to grab him, and he just runs all the harder—knows I'm playin'.

"Look at the exercise their legs are getting, Judd," I say. "That'll make 'em all the stronger; they'll go up hills like nobody's business."

He points to his own leg, out of the cast now, but still weak. "Maybe I should get in there with 'em," he jokes.

Not no accident that each of his neighbors has a little something to say to Judd, things like: "Well, we're returning your black and white better-tempered than it was before," and, "Think we put a little meat on their bones; they look better fattened up some, don't you think?" and, "You treat these dogs right, Judd, you'll get many years of good hunting from them."

I wish they'd just leave; Judd don't need no sermon right now. But I know he figures he owes 'em something, so he just nods, and after a time they go home. Then Judd and me sit on his back steps watching those dogs enjoyin' themselves, and I sure do feel good. Still, can't help glancin' at

Judd's hands now and then and wondering, Those the hands of a killer? He the one who done it?

When I get home and tell Dad about Judd getting his dogs back, I can see he's feeling good, too. Glad to be on neighborly terms with Judd Travers again, no hard feelings between them.

Ma's not feeling too good, though.

"Tooth is actin' up again," she says.

"You ought to go have it looked at," Dad tells her.

"Well, the pain comes and goes. I got some oil of clove on it now," she says.

One thing about Ma, she sure hates to go to the dentist. Dad says he don't know how a woman who can stand giving birth to three children is so afraid of the dentist, but Ma says there's no comparison. Children you ask for; toothaches you don't.

What I'm thinkin' is that Ma's been hurting since yesterday—I could see it in her eyes, but didn't say nothing. I give more time to Judd Travers, who, if he's not ninety-nine percent evil is sixty percent at least, and paid no mind to her at all.

"I'll read to Becky tonight," I tell her, when Becky's beggin' for a story. Ma nods and hands me the book. So Becky, still scratchin' her pox, crawls up on my lap, Shiloh beside us. When Becky leans her head back against me and sits real quiet, one hand resting on mine as I turn the page, I can understand why Ma would go through pain to have children and still not like the dentist. Of course, she give birth to Dara Lynn, too, but that's somethin' else entirely.

Becky and Dara Lynn go off to take a bath together, and Ma gets out the quilt she's makin' and settles down in front of the TV with Dad. I finish my homework at the table. We give up on Pilgrims, and we're studying about Alaska now; I'm reading how it gets as cold as seventy-six degrees below in winter.

I try to figure how cold seventy-six degrees below is. Wonder if you spit, would it freeze before it hit the ground? After the lights are out and I crawl under my blanket on the couch, all that coldness gets to me. When I hear Shiloh's toenails clickin' about on the porch, I feel my way to the door in the dark to let him in; he makes one fine back-warmer.

As I close the door again, I see this little beam of light movin' way off in the direction of Middle Island Creek. Can't place where it is exactly, but it's there sure as I got eyes in my head. It's sort of bobbing around, like somebody's holding a flashlight. I watch for fifteen, twenty seconds, maybe, and then the light goes out.

Eleven

It's the next day on the school bus I tell David about the light. And even though it probably don't mean spit, David Howard can work up one heck of a story with it, I know.

"Like a signal or something?" he asks, eager.

"Well, it could have been," I say.

He's cautious, though. "How do you know it wasn't just somebody with a flashlight out jogging after dark?"

"It was movin' too slow for that. And didn't stay on more'n fifteen seconds."

"Like somebody looking for something?" asks David.

"Maybe."

"The other boot!" whispers David. "We found one, and now Judd wants to find the other."

"David, that don't make any sense at all!" I tell him. "Why would the killer leave a body out in plain sight, but go hide the shoes somewhere else?"

71

"The murder weapon, then," says David. "Maybe Judd buried it somewhere along Middle Island Creek, and now that the police are looking for it, he wants to be sure it stays buried."

I lean back against the seat and stare out the window, wondering if David could be right. The sheriff hasn't found enough evidence to arrest Judd, but everybody from here to Wheeling is ready to string him up, it seems. Maybe they got good reason.

"Besides," says David, lookin' over at me, "if somebody's looking for something, why would they go out at *night?*"

"That's what I'm *tellin'* you! We got a mystery on our hands. But it don't mean it's anything to do with Judd," I say. Deep inside, though, I'm thinkin' maybe it does.

What's fun is sitting in Miss Talbot's class, me and David, and having this secret. During math, we pass these notes back and forth.

How high off the ground was the light? writes David.

How in the world would I know that? I wonder. It was dark—couldn't even tell where the ground was. But I write back, *Three feet, maybe four.*

Then it was a man holding the flashlight, answers David. *If it had been a kid, it'd be more like two or three feet from the ground.* I tell you, he can find clues in almost anything.

"Marty?" says Miss Talbot.

"Three," I say, staring at the blackboard where she's pointing. I don't even know what the question is.

Somebody snickers.

"What I'm asking," says the teacher, "is whether you would multiply or divide."

"Multiply," I tell her, making a guess.

"Correct," she says, and I let out my breath real slow.

On the bus going home, David says he'll ask his ma if he can stay at my house this weekend. That way we can take turns watching for the light. So when I get home with Dara Lynn, and Shiloh comes dancin' and wigglin' down the drive to meet us, I'm not surprised to hear the phone ringing soon as I step inside.

"Mom says it's your turn to come to our house," David tells me. "I can't sleep over there till you come here."

I ask Ma can I spend the night at David's.

"I think it's his turn to come here," she says.

"He was just here!" I say.

"Not to spend the night," she says. Nothin' is ever simple with mothers.

"Well, I can't go down there till you sleep here," I tell David.

Finally Ma says I can go to David's house for an overnight if David will sleep over the weekend after that. And on Friday morning, I put my toothbrush and pajamas and some clean underpants in my book bag before I leave for school.

"You be polite at the Howards' now," Ma says as she hands me a plate of fried cornmeal mush, cut in slices, crisp around the edges. I slather on the margarine and then the hot syrup.

"Why don't anybody ever invite *me* to sleep over?" gripes Dara Lynn, glaring down at her fried mush.

"'Cause you're a sourpuss, that's why," I tell her.

On the way to the bus stop, Dara Lynn says to me, "I wish you'd get run over and your eyes pecked out by crows."

"I wish you'd fall down a hole and pull the dirt in after you," I say.

If Shiloh hears the meanness in our voices he sure don't

show it. Happy as can be trottin' along beside us till he sees that school bus comin' to take us away.

"See you tomorrow, boy," I tell him, give him a hug.

Somebody on the school bus is passing out Gummi Bears, though, and Dara Lynn revives in a hurry. Sitting there beside a girl in third grade, eating Gummi Bears and swinging her legs, Dara Lynn don't look like such a poor neglected child to me.

Fred Niles gets on, and he's got a story to tell. Seems that somebody walked right into their house the day before and stole two jackets and a shotgun.

"Just walked right in while you were home?" asks Sarah.

"Ma was only gone two minutes," says Fred. "She walked down to the road to check the mailbox, and later we discovered what all was missing. We're locking our doors and windows from now on. Never had to do it before."

"Wouldn't surprise me if Judd Travers had something to do with it," says Michael Sholt. "Heard he got his cast off this week. Bet he's making up for lost time."

I got this feeling Michael may be right. But I say, "Could have been anyone at all."

"You know anybody else around here who would walk in a neighbor's house and steal from him?" Michael asks.

At school, we are so deep in Alaska I don't see we can ever get out. We're buying and feeding imaginary sled dogs for math, figuring how many pounds of food per day they're going to eat, and how many pounds they can pull. We're studying Eskimo paintings in art, and listening to Eskimo folktales, and for spelling I got to memorize words like "tundra," "Aleutian," "glacier," "petroleum," and "permafrost." Now I *know* I never want to feel what seventy-six degrees below zero is like.

I get off at David's house after school. David has his own key. His ma gets home a half hour after he does, and she's got a pile of papers to grade.

"Hi, Marty," she says. "There's chocolate pudding in the refrigerator if you boys want a snack."

"We already found it," David tells her.

I guess maybe everybody feels more comfortable at his own table in his own house. I know I feel a little awkward at David's. First off, there's always a tablecloth. I can't imagine a cloth on our table at home. Becky would drop spinach on it first off, and Dara Lynn would spill her milk. The Howards have napkins, too. Cloth napkins. And everything's in bowls that you pass around. Ma just sets a pan right from the stove on our table; it keeps the food hot, you want some more.

David's folks are nice, though. David and I tell his dad how we're studying Alaska, and he tells us about this dogsled race they hold up there every year called the Iditarod, and how you have to travel a thousand miles and sleep out in the snow and be careful your dogs don't drop off the ice and I don't know what all.

"You see much of Judd Travers these days?" Mr. Howard asks me finally when David's ma brings out the dessert.

"Some," I tell him.

"Wonder how he takes to all this talk of the murder."

"Don't take to it at all, same as you or me," I tell him.

Mr. Howard grows quiet after that.

Later we're lyin' on our backs on the top bunk in David's room, trying to make out the constellations on his ceiling. David and his dad got a package of those stick-on stars and planets, and they put them in just the right places so that the ceiling looks something like the sky would look if you stepped outside at night a certain time of the year.

"That's Orion, the Hunter," says David, pointing. "See those two bright stars there in the middle, and then the three bright stars below? Well, the two stars are supposed to be his shoulders, and the three stars are his belt."

Now who figured that out, do you suppose? How do they get a whole man out of five little stars? Why couldn't those two stars on top be the eyes of a wolf or something, and the three below be his mouth? Makes as much sense to me as a hunter.

And then, because we're talking about hunters, maybe, David says, "I'll bet it *was* Judd Travers who stole those jackets and that shotgun from Fred's house."

I roll over on my side, trying to see his face in the dark.

"How come whatever happens has to be Judd's fault?" I ask. "How come it all goes back to him?"

David thinks about that a minute. "I guess it's because anything that happened around here before was usually Judd's fault. The way he'd cheat Mr. Wallace over at the store. We've both seen him do that. Give him a ten-dollar bill, then get to talking, and when he got his change back, say he gave Wallace a twenty. Driving drunk and knocking over people's mailboxes. Kicking his dogs. Other people have done one of those things maybe once in their lives, but Judd can do all those things in a single month!"

"Yeah, but what if he's changed?" I say.

David thinks about that, too. "Maybe," he says. "But once you get a reputation, it follows you around like your shadow. That's what Mom says, anyway." He's quiet a moment. Then he tells me, "Mom said I can't come to your house anymore unless we promise not to go anywhere near Judd's."

Right then I see how I got connected in people's minds with Judd Travers.

"You haven't gone with me to his house since last fall,"

76

I tell David. "We can keep on not going there together. I don't care."

"I just wanted you to know," says David.

Next thing they'll suspect *me* of murder!

"You know, Marty, if he *did* have anything to do with killing that man, he could go to jail for a long time and you probably wouldn't have to worry about him ever again," David says.

I think about that awhile. Why *don't* I wish Judd would be found guilty? Why don't I wish he'd get sent to jail? David's right. It sure would solve a lot of problems, just like that. I wonder why I been trying so hard to take his side?

Because I think I know how Judd got to be the way he is, that's why. Once you know what happened to someone as a little kid, it's hard to think of him as one hundred percent evil. If Judd's the way he is because of what his dad done to him, though, maybe his *dad* was that way on account of what *his* dad done, and maybe the grandpa was that way because *his* father. . . . When's it going to end?

Dad picks me up early the next day before he starts his mail route and takes me down to the vet's in St. Marys. I'm stacking twenty-pound bags of cat box litter when John Collins comes in to scrub his hands, getting ready to operate on a collie that was hit by a car. The vet scrubs with a brush, even under his fingernails.

"What's happening up in Shiloh these days, Marty?" he asks me. "I've had two customers come in this week telling me that their homes have been broken into. Walk-ins, more like it. Somebody coming in when they weren't home, and helping themselves to whatever they want."

"You must be talking about Fred Niles's family," I say. "They got a shotgun and some jackets missing."

"No, hadn't heard about them. But one family's missing two twenty-dollar bills they kept on a shelf in their kitchen, and a woman tells me she came home to find half the food in her refrigerator gone. Drove her husband to work, she says, and came back to find a whole roast chicken, half a cake, and a pan of scalloped potatoes missing."

"Who do they figure took it?" I ask.

"Nobody knows. There's talk about Judd Travers doing it. Of course, as I said to Mrs. Bates, it could be more than one person. Could be a whole ring of housebreakers. I sure don't like to hear about that shotgun, though. Walking in a house when no one's there and helping yourself to a chicken is one thing; walking in with a gun, if they start using that shotgun, is something else."

Doc Collins puts on his surgical gown and then his gloves, and goes into the operating room. I go on with my stacking. Maybe it's me who's got his head in the sand, I'm thinking. Maybe I just don't want to face the fact it could be Judd. How long's he had that cast off now? Three days? And when did the robberies begin? Three days ago, exactly.

Twelve

David's got an idea about the light I saw over near the bridge. If Judd didn't murder the man from Bens Run, he says, maybe someone's trying to murder Judd.

He slips this note to me during history:

1. Let's say Judd didn't murder anyone, but suppose he knows who did?

2. What if the light you saw was the real killer's flashlight? I'll bet you he knows Judd could squeal on him, and he's setting a trap for Judd down by the creek.

I turn over my spelling paper and send a note back to David:

1. I think you're nuts.

2. I think that whoever the killer is, Judd or anyone else, he threw his murder weapon down the creek bank, and now he's trying to find it before the police do.

I remember how David says he wants to be either a forest ranger or a biologist. I write a P.S.:

P.S. I don't think you're going to be a biologist or forest ranger either one. I think you are going to write detective stories. Bad ones.

David reads my note and laughs.

"David," says Miss Talbot. "May I see that note, please?"

I don't move. I can feel the color rise to my face. David don't move, neither. He sure don't want Michael Sholt and the whole sixth-grade class knowing about that light I saw and snooping around the creek themselves.

"I . . . I can't," he says. "It's . . . it's not my note to give."

"Who wrote it?" asks the teacher.

Now the whole class is watching.

"I did," I say.

"Then may I see the note, please, Marty?"

I swallow and shake my head. Everyone's staring.

"It's . . . private," I tell her. This is a real good secret David and I have going, and Miss Talbot just might pin it up on the bulletin board, the way she did Jenny Boggs's note last week.

"I see," says Miss Talbot. "And is this class a private place?"

"No, ma'am," I say.

"Then, because you were taking school time for private business, I suggest you stay in after lunch and use some of your personal recess time for your studies," she says.

That's fair enough, I guess. I see David stick the note in

his pocket. So while the other kids are playing kick-ball out on the playground, I've got to make a list of Alaska's natural resources and David's got to list the mountain ranges. Why do we have to study Alaska in January? I wonder. Why couldn't it be Hawaii? The only thing we've got to look forward to is the next weekend, first of February, when David gets to stay overnight at my place.

That night when I go to the door to let Shiloh in, I see the light again. Feel so cold inside my body it's like I had ice cubes for supper. Now I know this mystery's real, not just something David Howard and me put together to have some fun. Somebody's out there in the night doing something he don't want nobody to see. Looking for something he don't want nobody else to find, I'll bet. Maybe even studying our house like I'm studying the light from our window, standing in the dark. Is it the killer? Is it Judd?

I stay at the window watching till the light disappears, trying to figure just where it's coming from, but when there's nothing but blackness outside your window, you got nothing to pin it to. The old gristmill seems the most likely place.

Turns out David can't come for a sleep-over that weekend, though, on account of we're not home. We got to go to Clarksburg for Grandma Preston's funeral on Saturday.

"It was pneumonia," Aunt Hettie cries over the phone. Can hear her voice all over the kitchen. "It happened so fast! One day she had a cold, and the next thing we know it's pneumonia, and then she's gone—just like that. I should have been with her. I could have taken off work, and gone to that nursing home and stayed right by her bed. . . ." She cries some more.

"Now Hettie, don't you go blaming yourself for something you couldn't help in a million years," says Dad. "You did the best you could for Mother, and no one's faulting you now. We'll be there Friday evening, soon as I can get away."

"What about Shiloh?" I ask when my dad hangs up. Grandma Preston's dead, see, and first words out of my mouth are about my dog.

"I'll ask Mrs. Sweeney to come by and feed him," says Ma.

"But the whole family's never been gone overnight before," I say. "Shiloh might figure we're not coming back." All I can think of is that a lot can happen to a dog in twenty-four hours.

"Marty, that dog of yours is rompin' all over creation with that Labrador, and he won't even miss you," says Dad.

"Couldn't we just put him in the house?" I beg.

"And ask Mrs. Sweeney to let him out every few hours for a run?" says Ma. "What if he doesn't come back when she calls him, and her with that bad knee? It's enough she's asked to feed him."

There's not much to say after that.

Ma spends the rest of the week cooking food for the funeral dinner. "Here's one thing I can do for Hettie," she says, wrapping up a ham and a dish of sweet potatoes.

Dad tells the post office why he won't be in on Saturday, and I call Doc Collins. By five o'clock Friday evening, we're on our way to Clarksburg, and Ma's in the front seat, trying to answer our questions.

Dara Lynn's just told Becky we aren't going to see Grandma Preston ever again. "Not ever, ever, ever, ever, ever," she says.

"Why?" asks Becky.

" 'Cause she's dead," says Dara Lynn.

82

"What's dead?"

"It's when your body gets as cold and stiff as an icicle and somebody could put a red-hot iron on your leg and you wouldn't feel nothing," Dara Lynn says.

"Dara Lynn, shut up," I tell her.

Becky asks if *she's* ever going to die, and Dara Lynn says yes, and Becky starts cryin', says she don't want nobody putting a red-hot iron on her leg.

"Becky," Ma says from the front seat, "your grandma's gone to be with the angels, and there won't be anymore sickness or pain for her ever again. We can rejoice in God's love."

"She won't be stealin' nobody's false teeth anymore, neither," says Dara Lynn, and we can't help ourselves. Have to laugh. We all feel better after that.

We sit up late that night talking to all the people who drop by Aunt Hettie's to remember Grandma Preston, and we sit real quiet through the service at the church next day. Dara Lynn keeps her hands to herself and Becky hardly makes a peep. I'm beginning to think Dara Lynn's not gonna be too bad a sister after all, but when we get to the cemetery, I wish she'd never been born.

She's standin' there beside me at the grave while the preacher reads from the Bible, the coffin resting on one side of the hole, waiting to go in. But when the preacher asks us to bow our heads and begins his prayer, Dara Lynn inches right over to that hole and peers down inside. I can't believe it!

"Dara Lynn, get back here!" I hiss.

Just then the dirt gives way, her being so close to the edge. Dara Lynn's arms start goin' around like a windmill, and somehow, though one leg went over the side, she lands on her knees and keeps from goin' in. She just don't have any sense at all when it comes to danger.

Ma reaches out and grabs that girl and yanks her back beside us—Dara Lynn's white socks all dirty now and mud on both hands. I'm thinkin' what I said about how I wish she'd dig herself a hole and fall in, but my mind don't stop there. I'm thinking how what if nobody saw her, and what if she really did fall in, a whole pile of dirt on top of her, and then the coffin goes in and Dara Lynn's buried alive.

It's such an awful thought I can feel the sweat trickle down my back. Sometimes a thought comes to you that you just can't help, but you don't go to jail for *thinking!*

And then we're all back at Aunt Hettie's, and it's like a picnic supper. Everybody's bringin' more food—sliced cheese and a turkey, and little rolls to fold the meat up in. There's potato salad and cherry pie and burnt sugar cake and marshmallow Jell-O. Can't tell if this is a party or a funeral.

It's near ten o'clock when we get home that night. First thing I look for is my dog, but this time I can hear him before we even turn up the drive. He is barking his head off, and when we get out of the Jeep, he don't even come over—just stands back there by the henhouse, his nose toward the woods, his body jerking with every bark he makes.

"Shiloh!" I say, and he comes over to give me a lick, then goes right back to barking again. Even after we take him inside, he's jumpy. Goes from one window to the next.

"What in the world has got into that dog?" asks Ma.

She checks out the house. Our TV is still there—the money box, Dad's shotgun. Nobody's made off with the toaster or the radio or anything else that we can see.

"I'm going to get my lantern and have a look outside,"

Dad says. He takes a flashlight, puts his coat on again, and goes to the shed.

But a few minutes later he's back. "The lantern's gone," he says. "Somebody took my shears and my knife, too. If it weren't for Shiloh, that thief probably would have broken into the house."

I had goose bumps on my arms before, and now even the goose bumps have goose bumps. Was it because of Shiloh's barking that the thief didn't come in, or was it that we turned up the drive just about then? And if we *hadn't* come home when we did, would the robber have made off with Shiloh, too?

"Oh, Ray!" says Ma, and sits down hard on a kitchen chair. They stare at each other. "It's like someone knew we were gone."

"Well, I didn't go around telling everybody—just my supervisor at the P.O.," says Dad.

"I only told Mrs. Sweeney so she'd feed the dog," says Ma. "And Marty called the vet and David Howard, but that's all."

They stare at each other some more, and Dad don't even blink. "Only other person who saw us leave was Judd Travers," he says at last. "We passed his pickup just after we pulled out of the drive."

Thirteen

And then the blizzard comes. We go back to school on Monday, the TV talking three inches of snow, but by the time the bus lets us off that afternoon, it's five or six, and still comin' down.

"We gonna be snowed in!" Dara Lynn crows happily, dropping her coat on the floor.

Becky looks worried, but Dara Lynn grabs her hands and dances her round and round the kitchen, tellin' her how we might not have to go to school for a whole week. Then Shiloh gets into the act, skidding around the linoleum, his toenails clickin' and scratchin'.

"Well, I sure wish I'd got extra milk," says Ma. "I can always make bread, and I've got beans and salt pork enough for an army, but there's not much substitute for milk."

"We can always put snow on our cereal!" says Dara Lynn, laughing.

Ma decides to get in the spirit of things, too, so she gets out her valentine cookie cutter, and she and the girls make cookies while I carry in wood for the little potbellied stove in the living room. Our house has a furnace, but it don't work if the electricity goes out, so a couple years back Dad put in the potbellied stove.

"Next best thing to a fireplace," Ma says.

I know if I don't bring in the wood now and stack some more on the porch, I'm not going to be able to find the woodpile in another couple hours.

Shiloh goes out with me, and tries to tunnel through the snow with his nose. I stack wood on the porch first, then stamp the snow off my boots and make another couple trips from the porch to the stove inside. By this time Shiloh's had his fill of snow and comes when I call. He plops down close to that potbellied stove, giving out big contented sighs, his eyes closin'. He wore himself out.

Every time there's another report on TV about the blizzard nobody knew was comin', the weather bureau moves the number of inches up. Twelve to fifteen inches of snow, one of the weathermen says now, and, a half hour later, he's talkin' two feet.

Dad finally gets home about eight, and can hardly make it up the drive. He's got snow tires on the Jeep and four-wheel drive, but the wind's blowin' the snow in drifts across the road. I can tell by the look on Ma's face when she hears that Jeep that it's about the best music in the whole world to her.

Dad's real pleased to see all the wood I brung in.

"Good for you, Marty," he says. "Last I heard, we're goin' to need every stick of it. They're talking thirty inches now."

Dara Lynn squeals some more.

I wake up next morning and look out the window in

87

sheer wonder. Dad's stomping back in the house to say that he can't move the Jeep one inch—he'd have to shovel all the way down to the road, and then couldn't go anywhere. Plow hadn't been down there, either.

"Well, Dara Lynn, looks like you got your wish," Ma says, turning the French toast over in the skillet.

It's only the second time in all the years Dad's worked for the post office, though, that he hasn't been able to get his Jeep through, and he worries about people who are waiting for their pension checks.

"Even if the checks got through, nobody could get to a bank to cash them," says Ma.

David calls, of course, and tells me they haven't been plowed out yet down in Friendly, either, and his dad is still trying to get to the newspaper office. Then Ma calls Aunt Hettie in Clarksburg to make sure she's okay, and finally there's nothin' else to do but give in to being snowbound.

Snow finally stops about noon, and Dad goes out with a yardstick to measure where it's flat in the yard. Thirty-one and a half inches, not counting six or seven feet along the side of the house and shed where it's drifted. We shovel a path to the henhouse to get some feed to the chickens.

Us kids have to go out in it, of course. I take a shovel and dig a path from our porch to a tree, just so Shiloh can do his business. Dara Lynn and Becky, fat as clowns in their snowsuits, scarfs wrapped around their faces, only their eyes peeking out, set to work diggin' a cave at one side of my path, but Becky no sooner sits down inside it than the roof falls in on her. She's squallin', looks like she got hit in the face with a cream pie, and I got to carry her into the house. I sure wish David Howard was here. We'd dig a tunnel all the way down to the road.

We have a fine time—go out and come in so many times that Ma just puts our caps and mittens beneath the potbellied stove to dry out, so they'll be ready again when we are. House smells like wet wool and Ma's home-baked bread. Dara Lynn's cheeks are red as apples, her nose, too. She wouldn't be half bad-lookin' if she'd just keep her mouth shut.

By middle of the afternoon, though, Dad's gettin' calls sayin' that trees are down, and power lines as well. The snow's wet and heavy, like pudding, and plows can't get through till the trees are cleared off the roads. They got a substitute mail carrier deliverin' what mail he can down in Friendly, and I know Dad wants in the worst way to be doin' his own route. A matter of pride.

Ma's cheerful, though. Says we can toast marshmallows in the woodstove after supper, and then we watch a *National Geographic* special on alligators. But fifteen minutes from the end, the TV goes out along with the lights.

"Hey!" yells Dara Lynn. "What happened?"

"What do you suppose?" I say. "The electricity went off."

"Ray . . .?" says Ma.

Dad makes his way into the kitchen to get the flashlight. "Well," he says, "I imagine a transformer went out somewhere. Guess we're lucky it waited till we had our supper."

We hang round the stove till the fire dies down. Dad don't want to put in any more wood, in case the power's off a long time, and we need every bit of wood we can find.

"Why don't we go to bed early to stay warm, and maybe the electricity will come back on in the night," says Ma, and she gets out some candles to make an adventure of it. The girls go to bed without their baths, because we all got wells out this way, and the electric pump won't bring up the water

89

if the power's off. The only water we got for drinking and cooking is what's left in the water heater right now.

Shiloh and me are lucky. Because the woodstove's in the living room, and we're sleepin' on the couch, we got the warmest place of all. But when we get up the next morning, the house is cold as an ice chest. Dad's got his coat on over his pajamas, and he's bringing in wood from the porch to feed the stove.

Ma tells me to dress without washing up, and nobody's to flush a toilet. Dara Lynn immediately sets up a howl.

"It's gonna stink in there!" she cries. "I ain't going to use no toilet that stinks!"

Ma turns on her suddenly. "Dara Lynn, I can think of a hundred worse things that could happen to you, and I don't want to hear another word. You don't want to use the bathroom, you can potty in the snow."

That shuts Dara Lynn up in a hurry. I smile; can't help myself—just thinking of Dara Lynn with her backside in a snowdrift. But I can see right off that today's not goin' to be near as much fun as yesterday. The woodstove's got a round top on it, not made for cookin', so Ma puts a pot over it upside down, and grills our toast on its flat bottom. Everything takes twice as long to make, though, and finally, cold as we are, we settle for Cheerios and the last of the milk. It's right about then we hear the sound of an engine grinding out on the road somewhere.

"Snowplow!" sings out Dara Lynn, looking toward the window.

No sight of anything, though. Don't look like there's any plow comin' along the country road. And then we see Judd's pickup, a plow blade in front, turnin' right up our driveway.

Slowly, his wheels spinning, Judd pushes his way

through the snowdrifts till he can't go no more, then backs up and makes another run at it. We all go to the window to watch, and Dad steps out on the porch and waves.

The pickup keeps comin', huge mounds of snow moving ahead of it. Every so often, Judd turns the wheel, ramming into the snowbanks with the plow to get rid of his load. The snow sure isn't doin' his truck any good, but Judd keeps at it, pushin' a little bit farther each time before he backs off and makes another run. Finally he gets up as far as our porch.

"Judd, I sure do appreciate this," Dad calls.

Judd rolls down his window. "Thought you might need to get out."

"Won't you come in and warm up?" Ma calls.

"Couple more folks I got to help out," Judd yells. "Thanks, anyway." And he makes a wide sweep to turn himself around, then heads off down the driveway, pushing more snow in front of him.

If people would just give him a chance! I'm thinking. See how much he's changed! But at the same time, I'm wondering is that a new jacket he's wearin'? And is that shotgun I see resting above the back window in the truck really his?

Fourteen

By next day, the electricity's still off, and we all sleep on the floor in the living room around the stove. Dad brings in a pail of snow and sets it by the toilet to flush it, but the bathroom's so cold the snow don't thaw. Now we got buckets of snow settin' all around the stove, coaxin' it to melt. Only good thing we've had to eat is hot dogs, 'cause you can put 'em on a stick and shove 'em right in the fire.

Dad gets out his Jeep to see how far he can go, but this time he's stopped by a tree that's down. Trees and wires all the way between here and Little, and when he tries to go the other way, across the bridge and on past Judd's, he come to the place where even Judd quit plowin'. Big wall of snow blocking the whole road. Drifts clear up over Dad's head.

"Sure am glad I'm not expectin' a baby in a blizzard like this," says Ma. I see her hand go up to her jaw and figure she's thinking a toothache would be even worse.

The bad part is we can't get no news on the TV or radio, neither, and with the sky that sick color again, like it's going to throw up more snow, we don't much feel like rompin' around outside. Takes too long to warm up afterwards. Even Shiloh hangs back when we open the door.

And then things slide from bad to worse. Our phone line goes out.

I know Ma's thinkin' that if one of us had an accident or something, there'd be no way to call for help. No way for anyone to get in with an ambulance, either. Last year down in Mingo County, a man got hurt during a snowstorm and they had to send a helicopter to pick him up. Almost worth knockin' Dara Lynn off the roof just to see a helicopter set down in our field. I smile to myself, but you sure can't say a joke like that out loud.

Everybody's tired of snow. We're tired of eatin' cold food, tired of settin' on a cold toilet seat, and of everybody crowded together at night on the living room floor just to stay warm, gettin' on each others' nerves. Dad's the only one half cheery. He says just pretend we're campin' out, but I can tell he's itchin' to get to work, and Ma just plain wants out of the house. And as if that ain't enough, it starts snowin' once more.

But then, fast as things got worse, they get better. The power comes on during the night. We're all sound asleep when suddenly the TV starts blarin' and the lights come on. We sit up and cheer. Hear the furnace click. By morning the phone's workin', too, and about nine, we hear chain saws goin' out on the road, crews workin' to remove trees that are down, and then the low grinding sound of the snowplow.

Dad gets to work about noon. Weatherman on TV says

the four more inches of snow we got is all it will be for a while, and suddenly the world looks good again.

Weren't all the roads in the county cleared, though, so the schools stay closed till Friday. Then everyone's got stories to tell of just how bad the blizzard was at his place, and I make a point of telling how Judd Travers come and plowed us out; plowed out some other driveways, too. To hear me tell it, Judd was part Paul Bunyan and part Jesus Christ, doin' all kinds of hero and wonderful things. No one says a bad word against him this time, but I don't hear no kind word for him, neither.

And then that evening, I see the light again over near Middle Island Creek. I stand at the window in the dark watching, and get the feeling like something real bad is out there. Why's it staying right across from where we live? Why don't it go somewhere else? How do I know that after I go to sleep at night, that light won't come floating and bobbing right up our driveway and around our place? I'm glad David Howard's comin' to sleep over the next day. Sometimes I feel we got us a mystery I'd just as soon not have.

I go to my job at the vet's Saturday morning, and when Dad picks me up at noon, we stop by David Howard's and get him. As soon as we finish our lunch, we're going to explore the gristmill, where I figure that light's got to be.

This time, though, Dara Lynn wants to go with us.

"No way," I tell her.

"Why not?" she says.

" 'Cause we're doing our own stuff. You go do yours."

"I'll just watch," says Dara Lynn.

"You will not!" I yell, as she follows us to the door.

Ma comes out of the bedroom. "Dara Lynn, you got things to play with in here," she says. "I'll mix up some flour

94

paste, and you and Becky can cut pictures out of magazines, make a scrapbook."

"I don't want to make no scrapbook! I can play out in my own yard if I want!" Dara Lynn says.

David and I go out, but leave Shiloh inside so he won't give us away when we give Dara Lynn the slip. We're tryin' to beat her to the bridge, but we get halfway down the drive and here she comes, clomping along in her boots, not even buckled. So we have to make like we're going hiking along the creek in the other direction, hide behind some trees, then head back the other way using the same footprints in the snow to confuse her.

By now the thirty-one inches have sunk down to twenty or so, and melting all the time, but every step we take is still a high one. Finally we see Dara Lynn headin' back up toward the house, so we make our way toward the bridge, down the bank, and push our way through the tangle of bushes and trees and snow to the cinder block supports of the old mill.

The old white-shingled building is propped up on a dozen or so columns to keep it out of the water in flood season, and one whole side of it's been burned or collapsed out of sheer misery, can't tell which. Dad won't let us climb up in there—too dangerous—but we take a good look below.

We hold on to each other, 'cause we know that the ground slants toward the creek, and it's full of ruts and gullies. One wrong step, and we're in a snowbank over our heads. Can't even tell where the bank stops and the creek begins. You get thirty-one inches of snow falling down in this place, plus the four or five inches more, plus all the snow that blows off the road or was pushed down here by the plow, why . . . a person could get buried, and nobody find him till spring.

I take this old dead limb and dig out a path in front of us. Even without snow, it's hard to see just what's here. Imagine the waterwheel was on the side next to the creek, but we sure can't make out anything.

"Know what?" David says at last. "If anybody had been down here, either we'd find his footprints or he's buried at the bottom of this snow."

I stop and think. Without moving my feet, I twist my body all around, lookin' in every direction, and I don't see any footprints here at all, not around the gristmill nor the bank nor the path leading up to the road—only the tracks we made ourselves.

"Shoot!" I say, disappointed.

"If we dig, though, we might find a body under the snow," says David.

"Yeah," I say, not all that eager. We don't even know what we're lookin' for anymore—just talkin' nonsense. We both know we're not about to go back to my place, carry a shovel all the way down here, and start digging.

We claw our way back up the bank, same place we come down, and make a whole pile of snowballs—line 'em up on the bridge. Then we take turns seeing if we can hit a stick far out there on the ice.

We do a couple of throws, and I've just picked up my third snowball when suddenly there's this loud *whomp!*, like a whole house has rose up in the air and set down again.

David and I turn, starin' in the direction of the noise, just in time to see snow slidin' off the roof of the old Shiloh schoolhouse. We run over and wade through the school yard, and there's half the roof caved in, settin' there like it's been that way forever.

"Wow!" I say.

"It went just like that!" says David. "All that snow!"

"Let's check it out!" I tell him, and we go over and try the door. Locked, of course. Paint flecks scattered all about. Through the dusty window I can see an old refrigerator, a flowered armchair that the mice have nested in, some children's desks, a table. . . . We go around back to where the outhouse is. And then we stop dead still and stare, because there's a fresh path in the snow between the outhouse and a cellar window.

"Marty!" David whispers, his eyes half popped from his head.

We know what we're going to do. We check out the outhouse first, and my heart's like to jump out of my skin. The snow's been cleared away where the door's ajar, and I figure if anybody's in there hearing us talk, he'd probably pull the door to. But I know if we get up to that door and peer around it and see somebody sittin' inside, I will die on the spot.

We're lifting our feet so high with each step it looks like we're marching, and David gets to the door first.

Ready? he mouths to me. I nod. He hooks one finger around the edge of that door and slowly, slowly pulls it open.

Creeeaaak! it goes, just like in the movies.

"Whew!" I say, when I see the seat's empty.

Together, we turn and look at the school, knowing that somebody could be watching us that very minute. At the same time, we know as sure as we got teeth in our mouth that we're going to climb in there and take a look. You can see by that open window where somebody's been crawlin' in and out.

"Who's gonna go first?" asks David, meaning that he was the one who checked out the outhouse, and now it's my turn.

97

I get down on my knees, stick one leg inside, and back in. See that somebody's put an old bench below the window to step down on, and soon as both my legs are in, and then my back and head, I look around.

"What do you see?" David whispers.

"Junk," I tell him. "Broken-down chairs. An old blackboard. Rats' nests—pigeon poop." But I don't see a living soul. Don't hear a single sound except the creak of some boards where the wind blows through.

"Come on in," I say to David, and he climbs in, too. The floor above us is sagging, so we hug the wall wherever we can. Have to crawl over a ton of stuff to get to the stairs, and then we stick to the sides in case they give.

When we get to the top, we see where the roof's come down, spilling snow onto what's left of a classroom.

"David!" I say, and point. There is my dad's lantern, sittin' right on the floor beside a blanket. I'd know it anywhere—got a piece of tape at the back to hold the batteries in. We look around, and there's a shotgun, too. And some chicken bones and a box of crackers. Any minute now, I'm thinking, I'll feel a gun in my back.

I walk over to pick up Dad's lantern, but then my heart almost gives out and my legs start to buckle. All I can do is grab David's sleeve and point, 'cause there, sticking out from under one of the fallen rafters, with snow and shingles on top, are the curled fingers of a man's glove. And on down the pile of rubble, about where his foot would be, is half a man's boot showing.

Fifteen

Forget Dad's lantern. David and me tumble back down those steps, scrambling over junk in the basement, sure that any minute someone's goin' to snatch us by the ankles, pull us back. We get outside, and go floppin' and falling through the snow till we reach the road, then tear across the bridge and on up the drive, our breath comin' in steamy puffs.

We reach the house, scramble up on the porch, and we're both trying to squeeze through that door at once, falling over Dara Lynn's boots she's left right there on the rug.

"Marty, what . . .?" asks Ma, lookin' up from her sewing.

"Over in the schoolhouse . . ." I point. "The roof caved in from all the snow and there's a dead man under the rafters." I collapse on a chair, my chest heaving.

Ma rises from the sofa, her scissors sliding to the floor. "You sure 'bout this, Marty?"

99

"Sure as Christmas," says David, and we wait, starin' at each other while Ma makes the call to the sheriff.

Dara Lynn says she will never forgive us, not takin' her along.

"I never seen a dead person in my whole life!" she cries.

"You have too. You seen Grandma Preston," I tell her.

"I never seen one that got a roof caved in on him," she wails.

I am actually thinking of taking Dara Lynn over there and showing it to her, but Ma says David and me are not to go back till the sheriff gets here, and Dara Lynn's not to go at all. Not somethin' for a little girl to see. So we watch from the window, and when the sheriff's car shows up out on the road later, David and me go on over. They got a police dog with 'em.

Sheriff rolls down his window. "You the boys who found a body? Your ma called?"

I nod. I point to the schoolhouse.

Car moves on slow across the bridge, and David and me follow. We show 'em the path in the snow from the basement window to the outhouse, and one of the deputies points out another path leading off into the woods. David and I didn't notice that one at all.

"Okay, now," the sheriff says. "I want you boys to stay outside with Frank here while Pete and I go take a look." Frank's the man with the police dog, I guess.

David and I stand there watching, wondering how in the world Pete, the fat one, is going to get himself through that basement window—jacket, gun, belly, and all—but he does.

Frank lets us pet his dog while we wait. We can hear the other men talking inside, but can't make out the words.

Now and then a board creaks, something else giving way, I guess. Footsteps going back and forth across the floor.

After a while the men come out again, Sheriff crawling out first through that basement window, Pete behind him, dragging a leaf bag filled with stuff. I can see the shotgun sticking out of the bag. I tell 'em Dad's lantern is in there, but they say they've got to keep all the evidence for a while.

"So what you got?" Frank asks the others.

Sheriff grins at us. "Well, there was a glove and a boot, all right, but nobody in 'em. I'll admit, it sure looked like there was a body under there, but it was just some clothes."

But before David and I have a chance to feel really stupid, Sheriff says, "But look what else we found, Frank," and holds up a pair of bright orange pants.

Frank whistles, then smiles.

"Know what this is?" the sheriff asks David and me. "The uniform over at the county jail. We've been lookin' for those two escapees, and it appears this is where they've been."

My hand moves into my jacket pocket and deep down in one corner where I'd forgotten all about it, I find this piece of orange cloth that Shiloh and the Lab were playing with.

"There you go!" says the sheriff when he sees it. "Piece of the shirt! Where'd you find that?"

"My dog brought it home," I say, as David stares.

"Surprised they got this far," says Pete. "Probably dropped their clothes as soon as they could steal something else to put on their backs."

"Well, we figured they'd show up sooner or later, weather like this," says the sheriff, taking the piece of shirt in my hand and sticking it in the bag, too. "What I can't figure, though, is why two men, who only had thirty days to serve for disorderly conduct, would pull something like this. Walk off that work detail. Now they've got to serve even more time when we catch 'em."

"Heck," says Pete. "I'd choose jail just to stay nice and warm. Three square meals, a bunk and blanket . . . who knows what they were eating here!"

I'm wondering the same thing. I've been up to Middlebourne before with my dad, and the jail actually don't look too bad. Sort of like a castle snuggled there next to the courthouse, with the words, COUNTY JAIL in bright red letters. You put a wreath on the door, it'd look right cheery.

"But where are they now?" I ask.

"That's what Sergeant here is going to find out," Sheriff says, and he gives that dog a good healthy sniff of the jail clothes.

David and I watch as that dog buries his nose in the uniform, like he's drinking in the scent, and then he starts running around, nose to the snow. Pretty soon he's on the path to the outhouse and, after that, the path through the woods.

The story makes the next edition of the *Tyler Star–News*. There's a picture of the old Shiloh schoolhouse with its roof caved in, and the story says how two boys found the hideout. And then it tells how those men, who'd been arrested for disorderly conduct, turned out to be the chief suspects in the murder of the man from Bens Run. David was right about that much, anyway. They'd figured that the longer they were in jail, the better chance the sheriff had of connecting them to the killing, so they got away when they saw the chance. Seems they'd been gambling with the man from Bens Run, who owed them a pile of money, and when he said he couldn't pay them, they got in a fight. Whether they meant to kill him or not, the court, I guess, will decide.

The story says that the police dog found them a couple miles away, coming back through the woods with some more blankets and half a roast beef. Photographer wanted to come and take our picture, but Mr. Howard wouldn't let him. Dad wouldn't even let the newspaper use our names. Said he didn't especially want the men to know who the boys were who found the hideout, and where they lived.

But it felt pretty good to be a hero for a day—me and David both. Tell the truth, I'd forgot about those men escaping from the county jail, and never dreamed they'd got clear over to Shiloh lookin' for a place to hide.

The kids on the bus Monday morning want to hear all about it—don't take them long to figure out who the two boys were.

"It *was* you and David, wasn't it?" squeals Sarah Peters.

"You see 'em go in the schoolhouse, or what?" asks Fred Niles.

"They pull a gun on you?" Michael Sholt wants to know.

Tell the story all over again, but I guess I skim the truth a little by leavin' things out—like how David and me run like roosters when we saw that glove sticking out from under the rafter. But if I leave things out, David puts things in, and after he gets on the bus, each of us giving our account in our own way, we have a story rolling like you wouldn't believe.

One kid tells another, and he tells somebody else, each of 'em tacking on a little something, so that by the time the bus gets to school and the story reaches Miss Talbot, it seems David and me had trapped the vicious killers in the old Shiloh schoolhouse, and then we climbed up on the roof and tramped around so that it fell down, burying the men in snow up to their armpits.

But wouldn't you know, Miss Talbot made a lesson of it? She can make a lesson out of anything. First it's Pilgrims, then Alaska, and now we got to find out all about prisons—how many in the state of West Virginia, how you get there by doin' what, and how long you got to stay. Don't ever tell your teacher somethin' she don't need to know, or she'll make homework out of it quicker'n you can say, "My dog Shiloh."

Each time we tell the story, though, I say, "See? It wasn't Judd, after all! You had him all wrong. He's changin'! You should see all he's done for his dogs."

But the worst was right around the corner, and maybe, if I'd known what was comin' next, I wouldn't have said nothing at all.

Sixteen

Valentine's Day, and David and me get more valentines than any other boys in our class—most of 'em from girls. In sixth grade, we don't go much for valentines—just the gross and crazy kind—but here are all these hearts with our names on 'em. I even got a valentine from Sarah Peters with a stick of spearmint gum stuck to the front, and the words VALENTINE, I CHEWS YOU! Sarah Peters never give any boy a valentine before, namely 'cause she's so stuck on herself, and all because she can swim. On a swim team or something. But here's this big valentine with her name on it. Embarrassing is what it is, especially since I didn't give out any valentines at all.

On the way home, after David Howard gets off the bus, Dara Lynn comes and sits beside me. She's showin' me all her valentines, and then she reaches in her coat pocket and pulls out the one from her teacher. Got a whole Milky Way bar with a ribbon around it.

I can't believe her teacher gave everybody a big candy bar like that. Dara Lynn, of course, starts peelin' the wrapper off that chocolate real slow like, wavin' it around in front of my nose till I think I hate my sister worse'n spinach.

And then, all of a sudden, she breaks that candy in half and hands a piece to me. "Here," she says.

I look at the candy. Look at Dara Lynn. "That half got poison in it?" I say.

"No," she tells me, jiggling it a little. "Go on. You can have it."

I take the candy and look it over good. Seems fine to me. Take a bite. The purest, sweetest chocolate you ever did taste. Dara Lynn settles back in her seat, swingin' her legs and eatin' that chocolate bar, and I eat my piece, too, and think how if I live to be a hundred, I will never understand my sister.

Kids still talkin' about the men from the county jail hidin' out in the old Shiloh schoolhouse. All the stuff that they'd stolen was returned, and Fred Niles's dad got his shotgun and two jackets back.

"See?" I say to Fred. "You were accusing Judd for nothing."

"I'll bet he's taken stuff we don't even know of, though," Fred says.

I turn halfway round in my seat. "Why are you always tryin' to blame Judd for every little thing that happens?" I ask, angry.

But Sarah says, "The way he used to treat Shiloh, Marty, I'd think you and Judd would be enemies. Tell me one good thing he's done."

"He plowed us out after the blizzard. Plowed out a few more besides," I say, and try hard to think of something else.

Judd wasn't drinkin' anymore that I knew of. Wasn't knocking down anybody's mailbox. Wasn't going around stealing all the stuff people thought he had. Then I see that all I'm doing is thinking of things he *wasn't* doing. I was short on things he did.

"You know what I think?" says Michael Sholt, maybe jealous of all the attention David and me got that day. "I think you and your dad are afraid of him. No matter what he does, you say a good word. He's got you scared!"

Now I'm really mad. "Has not! I wasn't too scared to stand up to him and take Shiloh!" I say. "Dad wasn't scared to go tell him not to hunt on our land!"

"Well, *my* dad says the Traverses have been trouble ever since they been here—my granddad knew his granddad—and they are bad news, the whole lot of them! If a man goes driving around drunk, destroying people's property, you don't reward him by fixing up his truck and taking him food."

"But it worked, didn't it?" I say. "He's not driving drunk anymore! He didn't kill that man or rob those houses. What else do you want him to do?"

"Move to Missouri, as far from here as he can get," says Michael, and laughs. Sarah and Fred laugh, too.

At dinner that night, I tell Dad what Michael said.

"Well, Marty," he says, "a person's got to make up his mind: Does he want someone to change for the better or does he want to get even? And if you want to get even with somebody, you'll get back at him, he'll get back at you, and there's no stopping it."

"But I wish there was some way we could make people like Judd better," I tell him.

Dad don't answer for a moment. Puts a square of mar-

107

garine on his mashed potatoes and covers it all with pepper. "You can't *make* folks like you, Marty, and you especially can't make folks like somebody else."

I lay on the living room floor after supper over by the woodstove and wrestle with Shiloh. He had his head on my leg all through dinner, his big brown eyes watchin' every morsel of food that travels between my plate and my mouth, like why don't something make a detour down his way? And sometimes, when Ma ain't lookin', I'd slip him a piece of fat off my pork chop.

But now we both been fed, and Shiloh sure loves to romp after a good dinner. I lay down on the floor and hide my face in my arms, and that dog goes nuts. Tries every which way to roll me over, and finally he'll run his nose up under my arm and all down my side, and get to tickling me so I laugh and have to turn over, and then he's happy.

Ma's watching from over in her chair and smiling. "Maybe he thinks you're not breathing, Marty, lyin' so still. Maybe he's got to see you're still alive," she says.

Hard to tell sometimes if that dog's playin' or workin', but we roll around till we're both wore out, and then I lay still on my back and let him put his head on my chest. Stroke his ears and think how I must be one of the luckiest people in the whole state of West Virginia.

February turns to March, and every now and then we get a little taste of spring. Wind feels just a bit warmer. You walk outside and everywhere you hear the sound of running water. Snow sliding off the roof, ice melting on the shed, and all the extra water makes the creek run higher and faster, so the sound's louder than it was. Every day the heaps of dirty snow that the plow left at the side of the road get smaller and smaller, and now and then there's a good hard rain that almost melts it down while you watch.

In between the rains, the sun shines warmer and brighter, and all the water in the ditches and gullies shines back at you. Ma sees her crocuses starting to come up, and goes out to count them.

Judd works at Whelan's Garage every other Saturday, meanin' that every other week he's got the weekend off. Once in a while I hang around his place—help him wash his truck, maybe.

Can't say I see a huge change in the way he treats his dogs, but I see some. He don't cuss at 'em like he used to, and I don't see him kick 'em. Now and then he'll reach out to pet one of 'em, but they always shy away a little when he does that. Guess it's the same with animals as it is with people—takes them a long time to win back trust.

"I think your dogs are happier now that they got a yard to run in, don't have a chain around their necks," I tell him as I wipe the hubcaps on his pickup.

"Seem happy," Judd says. "Neighbors say they don't bark as much."

"Well, that's good, then," I tell him. "Fence holding up okay?"

"Yeah, but I wish I'd put a gate in it after all. When I'm in the backyard and want to go round front, I got to go in through the trailer first," Judd says.

"Well, we got the extra fencing behind your shed," I say. "Want me to help you put the gate on?"

"I'm going over to Middlebourne today, but you can come by tomorrow, you want to," Judd says.

"Sure," I tell him.

* * *

Sunday's on the cold side, but when the sun comes out from behind a cloud, the air takes on a different feel. Something about a March sun on the back of your neck, you *know* spring's not far off. Shiloh's out with the black Labrador somewhere, and I'm glad, 'cause we both seem to feel guilty when I head for Judd's—Shiloh, for not comin' with me, and me, 'cause I'm goin' somewhere without him. But today he don't have to watch me leave, and I tell Dad I'll be back soon as I help Judd put on that gate.

When I get to the trailer, Judd's dogs are having a fine time out in the yard. He's thrown 'em an old sock with a knot in it, and they are just chewin' it to pieces, growlin' and tugging and shakin' their heads back and forth, holding on with their teeth for dear life. Keeps 'em busy while we work on the fence. Judd's got pliers and a hammer, and he unhooks the wire from one of the poles. We roll it up and haul his gate into place. Got to move another pole over closer, and fasten some hinges on it.

It ain't as easy as it first seemed. I'm holdin' the gate upright and Judd's tryin' to hammer a pin down inside a hinge. His dogs are still at work on that sock, tumbling around and makin' like they're all so fierce. John Collins says that tug-o'-war's a game you shouldn't play with your dogs—makes 'em aggressive; turns 'em mean. But we done enough preaching already, and I'm not about to tell Judd how his dogs should *play*.

Suddenly—it happens so fast I almost miss it—Judd steps backward to test the gate, and the heel of his boot comes down hard on the left front paw of the black-and-white dog. Dog gives this loud yelp, Judd turns, lookin' to

110

see what's happened, and next thing we know, the black and white's sunk his teeth deep in Judd's leg.

Judd's bellowing in pain, I'm trying to call his dog off, the other dogs are barking, and a neighbor down the way opens her back door to see what's going on.

All the noise just seems to put the black-and-white dog in a frenzy. He's the biggest one of the lot, and he's tuggin' at Judd's leg like a piece of meat, growlin' something terrible. It's as though all the anger and meanness that dog's felt for Judd all these years is right now comin' up out of his mouth. Judd groans, swears, bellows again, tryin' to swing himself around, get the leg free, but he can't.

I'm about to run inside for a pail of water to throw on that dog when Judd lifts the hammer, hangs back a moment, then brings it down on the black and white's head.

The dog's legs give out from under him, his jaw goes slack, then he slumps to the ground and lays still.

111

Seventeen

I can't hardly breathe. Don't know who to head for, Judd or the dog, so I don't move at all.

"Clyde!" comes the neighbor's voice. "Judd Travers just killed that dog!"

That gets my feet moving. I go over to the black and white and put my hand on his chest to see if the heart's beating. Then I feel for the pulse on the inside of his hind leg, the way John Collins taught me. Nothing at all.

I look over at Judd. He's sittin' on the ground, arms on his knees, head on his arms. His pant leg's soaked with blood. The other two dogs have crept off to a far corner, just watching. Don't make a sound.

"Judd," I say, "you sit tight. I'm callin' Doc Murphy." And I run to the back door of his trailer.

"What's happened over there?" calls the neighbor's husband.

"Dog attacked Judd," I call back, but all the while I'm wondering, did he have to *kill* him? Judd's leg looks bad, though. Not the same leg that was broke, either. The other one. Now he's got *two* bum legs.

Doc Murphy says he's just about to walk out the door, going to visit his brother down in Parkersburg, and I say, "Doc, Judd's been hurt by one of his dogs and he's bleedin' pretty bad."

"Where you calling from, Marty?"

"Here at Judd's," I tell him. "He's out back."

I go out the door again. Judd is in the same position I left him, but he suddenly rears back and socks the fist of his right hand into the palm of his left just about as hard as a man can hit, cussing hisself out. Then he slumps again, and don't lift his head.

"Anything we can do?" the neighbor woman calls.

"Doc's on his way over," I yell back.

I sit down beside Judd. He's shakin' his head back and forth, back and forth, his shoulders twitching once or twice like he's about to hit himself again.

"My best hunting dog," he says. "Now I've lost two." I know he's counting Shiloh.

"This one ever do anything like that before?" I ask.

"Was always chained before. Don't know what got into him this time. I never meant to step on his paw."

"I know you didn't," I say.

He eases up his pant leg, and that is some bite. Big flap of skin just hanging there.

We hear a car coming down the road from the bridge, and it's not long before Doc Murphy makes a U-turn in front of Judd's and pulls his car off the pavement. Comes hurrying around to the back and walks through the opening

113

in the fence. Judd's other two dogs don't even bark. One of 'em's lying down now, head on his paws. Look like they're both too scared to move. They can tell something's happened to the black and white.

Doc Murphy grunts and sets his bag on the ground, then bends over Judd's leg and gives a whistle. His eye falls on the dead dog, blood oozing out one corner of his mouth, eyes fogged over. Sees the hammer, too, and shakes his head.

"You provoke that dog, Judd?"

"No, he didn't," I say, answering for him. "I seen the whole thing. Judd accidentally stepped on his paw. The dog bit him and wouldn't let go."

Doc sighs. "Well, we got trouble enough right here," he says. "Come in the house, Judd, where I can sew you up. Don't like to stitch up a dog bite if I can help it. Better to keep the wound open, keep it clean, but this one's going to take a whole bunch of stitches, I can tell you."

Seems like Judd just got through limpin' on one leg, and now he's limpin' on the other. I unwind that roll of wire fence back again and stretch it over the opening where the gate was to be so the other two dogs won't get out, and I fasten it good. Then I go inside. Soon as the yard's empty, I see the other dogs come over and sniff the black and white. One of 'em makes a whining sound in his throat. Don't tell me dogs don't cry!

I sit off to one side while Doc works on Judd. Got him sitting up on the table, leg stretched out on a towel where Doc can reach it. I get some more towels, and some hot water, scrub up good, and hand Doc things as he needs them.

"Okay, now, Judd," Doc says at last. "Don't want you to get that bandage wet. You come by in a couple of days, let me take a look at it, and we'll take the stitches out in two weeks or so. I got to pump you full of antibiotics now before I leave." He writes out a prescription, too. "And I got to take that dog with me; it's the law. Check him for rabies."

"Tell 'em I want him back," says Judd, real soft.

Doc turns around. "What you say?"

"I want the body back when they're done with it."

"Sure, Judd," Doc says. "I'll tell them."

I find an old box out back. Roll the dog's body into the box, and set it on the floor of Doc's car.

When he's gone, I go inside to wash up, see if Judd wants me to stay. He don't. He's on the couch, staring straight ahead.

Finally I tell him, "I'm sure sorry today turned out like it did."

But he don't answer, and I leave.

I tell my family what happened. Everyone's looking real sorry, even Dara Lynn.

Ma sighs. "Some people just seem to attract trouble," she says at last.

And Dad says, "Does seem like there should have been some other way to make that dog let go, but I don't know what. A dog get his teeth in you like that, he can tear you up mighty quick."

One good thing about bein' an animal is you don't have to know all the bad things happening around you. When Dara Lynn and me walk down to the school bus stop on Monday, Shiloh goes dancin' along beside us, frisky as you please. Don't even know one of his own kind was killed. But I see that all the sorry's gone out of Dara Lynn's eyes, too, and there's pure eagerness in its place.

"Listen here," I say. "I don't want you tellin' *any*body that Judd killed one of his dogs. Hear?"

"You can't make me not tell!" she says.

"If you tell what Judd did, I'll tell the whole bus how you threw up on your new shoes last summer," I say.

Dara Lynn's mad as hornets. "Okay!" she shouts. "I won't say he killed a dog!"

The bus comes and we get on, and the first thing out of her mouth is worse: "Judd Travers killed something yesterday!" And then, to me, "I didn't say *what*, did I?"

Fact is, couple of the kids had already heard, so the whole bus already knew.

"Just picked up a hammer and hit his own dog over the head. That's what his neighbor said," Fred Niles tells the rest.

"Listen!" I say. "I saw it happen. That dog was tearing up his leg. If Judd hadn't hit him when he did, he might not be walking now."

"Yeah, but why do his dogs hate him so much? Ask him that!" says Michael Sholt.

I worry a lot about Judd after that. Doc Murphy says he come by to have his stitches out, and the wound's healing nicely. The black and white didn't have rabies, the test showed, and as far as Doc knows, Judd's going to work every day. But when Judd's out in his truck and passes me on the road, it's like he don't even see me.

I go over once to ask if he wants to finish putting that gate on yet, 'cause the wire fencing's right where I left it, the gate swingin' in the breeze with no opening there at all. Judd's truck's out in front, but when I knock, nobody answers. I call, but nobody comes.

I go around in back to see if Judd's there. His two dogs

are inside the fence, but beyond that, out past his satellite dish, even, I see a little mound of fresh dirt at the edge of Judd's property. I walk back, hands in my pockets, and look down. There's a horseshoe stake driven in the ground at the head of this little grave, and around the stake is a dog's leather collar.

Eighteen

Seems like maybe we're back where we started with Judd Travers. Can't tell what's going on in his mind, 'cause he don't ever stop to talk to me. Saturdays I'll see him pass by out there on the road two, three times, but if I'm out there he don't even wave. Either he's mad at me, I figure, for bringin' that fence by in the first place, or he's grievin' for his dog.

Maybe all my work to be friendly and to give his dogs a better life is going to backfire, and when he looks at me, what he'll think about is how two of his dogs are gone.

"Just you stay away from him for a while," says Dad. "You got to give a man time to sort things through."

Closer it gets to April, the more it rains. Not a bit of snow left. Everything's mud, and just when you think there's not a drop of water could be left in the sky, it rains some more.

When it rains hard enough and long enough, Middle Island Creek overflows its banks and we get stranded. Being up the hill a ways from the road, our house don't get wet, but there's a stretch of road near the church in Little that floods when the creek is really high. "The Narrows," we call it, and Dad'll have to get to work another way. What we do is count the layers of stones in the supports that hold up the bridge here in Shiloh. If we can only see nine stones between the bottom of the bridge and the top of the water, we know the road down at Little will be flooded. More than nine, we're probably okay.

On Saturday when I go to the vet's, there's a litter of kittens somebody found along the creek. A mama cat had gone in one of those school bus shelters, no bigger than a phone booth, and had her babies, and the water was threatening to carry them off. She was meowing and somebody heard and brought 'em to John Collins. Hadn't even got their eyes opened yet.

I'm making sure each of those babies gets a turn at the mother's milk, and thinking how Dara Lynn wanted a kitten even before I wanted Shiloh. Can't believe I'm thinking what I am, but I say, "I'll take one of those kittens, Doc Collins."

"You get your pick, Marty," he says. "But you'll have to wait till they're eight weeks old. You don't want to take them from their mother too early."

Dara Lynn's got a birthday in May, and that'll be just about the right time to surprise her. But knowing my sister, she'll probably say something ugly—like how come she didn't get to choose it herself, or I got the wrong color. Sometimes you just have to take chances.

Somebody brings in a dog that morning to be checked

over 'cause he's tearing up the furniture. The man says that every time he comes home from work in the evening, the dog's destroyed something else.

I scratch the retriever's ears while John Collins talks to the owner—explains that dogs, like people, want a little more out of life than just hanging round waiting for somebody to come home, pay them some attention. They got to feel needed.

"Let your dog know that when you come home, it's his time, and you expect things of him," Doc says, "even if it's only to bring in the paper or chase the squirrels away from the bird feeder. Your dog wants to know he has a purpose."

The last Saturday in March, Dad picks me up after my job at the vet's and then we pick up David. Been raining all week, off and on, and the water's right high, lapping at the side of the road through the Narrows. When we get to the Shiloh bridge, we see there're only ten layers of stones showing on the supports between the floor of the bridge and the top of the water.

"It's close," Dad says.

He drops us off at the driveway and goes on to deliver the rest of his mail, and David and I run up to the house where Ma's got grilled cheese sandwiches and tomato soup waiting.

"Da-vid!" sings out Becky, all smiles, when she sees him. Girls always like to show off for David.

"Hi, Popcorn," says David.

Then Dara Lynn has to be her usual nuisance, and keeps kickin' us under the table and pretending it was Becky did it.

"Dara Lynn, will you stop it?" I snap, almost sorry I'm savin' that kitten for her.

120

"Dara Lynn, I'm not tellin' you again! Behave!" says Ma, and I notice she's holding her cheek. "I got no patience with you today." And then she gives this little half smile to David and says, "Sorry I'm not more cheery, but I got a toothache that is making my whole face sore."

I take a good look at Ma. "It's swelling up some, too," I say.

She feels with her hand, then goes and looks in the mirror. "Guess I ought to have gone to the dentist like your dad said," she tells me.

She goes back in the bedroom and lies down, and we try to keep it quiet in the living room. We spread out my Monopoly set on the floor and let Dara Lynn play, but when you get down on the rug like that, Shiloh thinks it's playtime, and he wiggles and rolls and tries to lick our faces, and soon the houses on Park Place are all over the board. Becky thinks it's funny, but Dara Lynn gets mad.

"Stupid old dog!" she yells, and hits at him hard. Shiloh gives this little yelp and comes around behind me. I swoop all Dara Lynn's houses and money off the board, and tell her the game's over. "Don't you ever, never, hit my dog!" I say.

"Oh, who wants to play Monopoly, anyway? Come on, Becky," she says, and the girls go off to their bedroom, get down the box of old jewelry Grandma Preston give them once, and try on all the pieces.

It's raining lightly outside, and David and me are waiting for it to stop. Then we're going back to the old Shiloh schoolhouse to see if we can find any more stuff those men left behind—keep it for a souvenir.

We horse around a little, try to teach Shiloh to help David take his jacket off, make himself useful. But Shiloh yanks too hard on one sleeve and a seam pulls out at the shoulder.

Ma comes out of the bedroom and makes some calls in the kitchen, then comes over to me.

"Marty, I've called the dentist and he says if I can get down there right now, he'll take me today. This toothache's gettin' worse and worse. I called Mrs. Sweeney, and she said she and her daughter are going to Sistersville and they think they can squeeze me in the cab of their pickup, too. Mrs. Ellison is going to come up here and watch you kids till I get back."

"We don't need a sitter!" I say, embarrassed.

"Maybe not, but the girls do, and I want you to behave for her now. Hear?"

She goes in the bathroom to brush her teeth, and by the time she's got her coat on, we can see Mrs. Sweeney's pickup coming up the drive. Ma goes out and gets in.

Great! I'm thinking. David comes for an overnight, and we get a baby-sitter! Mrs. Ellison's nice, though. Always leaves a little something in her mailbox for Dad when she bakes, and I'm thinking she might show up with a chocolate cake. At least Dara Lynn and Becky are having a fine time in their bedroom, and are leaving David and me alone for a change. We open a pop and watch a basketball game on TV.

Fifteen minutes go by, though, and Mrs. Ellison still hasn't come. Phone rings and she says, "Marty, your ma still there?" I tell her she's gone, and Mrs. Ellison says, "Well, the water here in Little is higher than I thought, and I'm afraid if I get over to your place in our Buick, I might not make it back again. Sam's on his way home right now, and he's going to drive me to your house in the four by four. Everything okay there?"

"Everything's fine," I tell her.

No sooner hang up than it rings again, and this time it's Michael Sholt.

"Marty!" he says. "I'm up at my cousin's, and there's a dead man floating down the creek! He just went by! Should be by your place in five minutes. Go see who he is!"

Nineteen

I drop that phone and David and me grab our jackets and run outside, Shiloh at our heels. The rain's tapered off, but there's mud everywhere. We don't care, though. We run up on the bridge and wait right in the middle, looking upstream. That is one wild-looking creek!

"You suppose dead men float on their backs or their stomachs?" I ask David.

"Stomachs," he says. "That's the way they do in the movies, anyway."

Who could it be? I wonder. Bet someone's called the sheriff already and there'll be men waiting down at the bend where the water slows—see if they can snag him, pull him in. Wouldn't it be something if David and me could find out who he is, and be the first to call the paper? And then the thought come to me: What if it's Judd Travers? Don't know what made me think that, but it just crossed my mind.

We stand out there on the bridge watching that muddy water come rushing at us and disappear under our feet. No one in the *world* would think Middle Island Creek was anything but a river now.

"You figure five minutes are up?" I ask David.

"Probably ten," he says. "What if Michael was kidding? Be just like him, you know. Get us standing out here on the bridge waiting to see a dead man, and him and his cousin laughing their heads off."

We stare some more at the water. You look at a river long enough, it makes you dizzy.

"There's something!" David yells suddenly, and I look hard where he's pointing. Sure enough, bobbing around the curve ahead is something about the size of a man. When it bumps a rock, we see an arm fly up.

"Jiminy!" breathes David.

We run to the far side of the bridge where it looks like the body is heading. Can't tell what color his hair is—can't even see his hair, just the shape of his head, and then his feet, tossing about on the current like the feet of Becky's rag doll.

"Here he comes!" yells David, just as I see Dara Lynn and Becky cross the road.

"Go on back!" I yell. "We're comin' right up." I turn toward the water again, and next I know, the body's coming smack toward us, sliding under the bridge, and we see it's no dead man at all, it's one of those dummies left over from Halloween.

"Ah, shoot!" says David, as we turn and watch it pop out from under the bridge on the other side, its straw-stuffed legs flopping this way and that. Even Shiloh's been fooled—runs across to the other side and barks.

"What was *that?*" Dara Lynn demands, hurrying over. She and Becky got their shoes on, but the laces are flopping, and Becky's jacket's inside out.

"It wasn't nothing—just somebody's Halloween dummy," I say. "Go on back to the house, I said!"

"Don't have to!" says Dara Lynn, sticking out her chin. "Ma didn't say I couldn't come down here. I can walk on the bridge same as you."

"We're all goin' back," I tell her.

But David's mad at Michael Sholt. "Bet he knew it was a dummy all along," he's grumbling. "Maybe he and his cousin dropped it in the creek themselves!"

Becky goes over to the edge of the bridge where the railing makes a diamond pattern. She's lookin' at a spiderweb strung in one of those openings. It glistens silver from the rain. I'm thinking that this water is rising faster than I ever seen it before, as though a couple more creeks have suddenly emptied into it up the way, and it's all of them together rushing under the bridge now.

"Come on," I say again, stopping to tie Becky's shoes for her. "We're goin' up to the house. Mrs. Ellison'll be along, wonder where we went."

Becky starts off again, Shiloh trotting ahead of her, and David catches up with me, talking about what he's going to do if Michael starts a story around that he saw a dead man in Middle Island Creek.

"Look at me!" sings out Dara Lynn behind us. I turn and see she's worked her head through one of those diamond openings in the railing, acting like she's a bird, going to sail out over the creek. Her big puffy jacket on one side of the opening, her head on the other, she looks more like a turtle. Girl can't stand not having all the attention on her.

126

"Dara Lynn, you cut that out and come on," I say. "Get on up to the house."

She just laughs. I grab her by the arm and pull her back through the railing just as the Ellisons' four by four turns in our drive and moves on up to the house.

"I got it!" says David. "If Michael says there was a dead man in the creek, we'll say we saw him, too. Only we'll make it different. Say it was a man with red hair and a blue shirt on."

I laugh. "His face all swole up. . . ."

"And he looked like he'd been shot in the heart!" says David. We both laugh out loud, thinking of Michael's face if we turn that trick around.

"'What'd I miss?' he'll be thinking," I say, "and . . ."

"Who-eeee!" I hear Dara Lynn whoop. I turn around and my heart shoots up to my mouth, 'cause right at our end of the bridge, Dara Lynn's climbed up on the railing, her skinny legs straddling it, one foot locked behind a metal bar to keep her balance. Both her arms are in the air, like kids do on a roller-coaster.

"Dara Lynn," I bellow, my voice cracking. "Get off there!"

She laughs, and in her hurry to climb up where I can't reach her, wobbles, grabs at the rail to steady herself, but misses. There's this short little scream, and then . . . then she's in the water.

"Dara *Lynn!*"

Stomach feels like I'm on a roller-coaster myself. Can't even swallow. I'm hanging over the rail, but Dara Lynn's too far down to reach. She's lookin' up at me with the wildest, whitest eyes I ever seen, her arms straight out at the sides like the cold of the water has paralyzed her. And then, just like the straw man, she disappears beneath the bridge.

David's shouting something, I don't know what, and Becky's run screaming up our driveway, then turns around and screams some more. I can see Mr. and Mrs. Ellison running down the drive toward her. David is running over to the railing on the other side of the bridge, his face as white as cream.

"Where is she?" he asks, turning to me. "She didn't come back out."

I am running around the end of the bridge, slipping and sliding down the bank toward the high water.

"What happened?" Mrs. Ellison calls.

"Dara Lynn fell in," I yell, and it's more like a sob.

"Oh, Lord, no!" cries Mrs. Ellison in the background, offering up a prayer for all of us.

All I can think of is havin' to tell Ma that Dara Lynn drowned. Of having to remember every last awful thing I ever said to her, like wishin' she'd fall in a hole and pull the dirt in after her. I am praying to Jesus that if he will save my sister I will never say a mean thing to her as long as I live, even while I know it's not humanly possible. "Just don't let her die, please, please!" I whisper. She'll drown without ever knowin' I gave her a kitten.

I squat down, lookin' under the bridge. I see that Dara Lynn's been snagged by the small trees and bushes sticking out of the water near the first support. At that moment she feels herself caught, and her arms come alive, floppin' and flailin' to turn herself around, and finally she's holding on, screamin' herself crazy.

Mr. Ellison's beside me now, and he's shouting instructions to Dara Lynn to pull herself hand over hand toward the bank, to grab on to the next branch and the next, and not let go on any account, while he wades out into that swirling water as far as he can to meet her.

It's when Dara Lynn pulls herself close enough for us to grab her that I think maybe the thumpin' in my chest won't kill me after all. But then it seems my heart stops altogether, for I see Shiloh out there in the water, the current carrying him farther and farther away. I know right off he jumped in to save Dara Lynn, and now he's got to save himself.

Twenty

All I hear is my scream.

We're haulin' Dara Lynn out, her clothes making a sucking sound as she leaves the water, but I can see my dog trying to paddle toward us; the current's against him, and he can't even keep himself in one place.

Most times Shiloh could throw himself into Middle Island Creek, chasing a stick I'd tossed, and come right out where he'd gone in, the water moves that slow. But when the rains are heavy and the creek swells fast, the water just tumbles around the bend, and Shiloh's never been in nothing like this before. He keeps tryin' to turn himself around in the water and get back to us.

"Shiloh!" I'm yellin', while behind me, back up on the road, Becky sets up a wail of despair.

"Oh, Lord Jesus, that little dog!" cries Mrs. Ellison, praying again, while her husband takes off his coat and wraps it around Dara Lynn. Dara Lynn's crying, too—huge sobs.

Is God puttin' me to some kind of test, I wonder—saving my sister and drowning my dog? Did I trade one for the other? Lord knows I can't swim. Oh, Jesus, why didn't you make me go to the park in Sistersville and take lessons with Sarah Peters? Why'd I get to sixth grade and not even know how to float?

My mouth don't seem connected to my head. Can still hear it screaming. "Shiloh! Shiloh!"

All he's doin' is tirin' himself out tryin' to swim back to us.

I slide farther down the bank, one foot in the water.

"Don't you try to go in there, Marty," Mr. Ellison shouts.

I claw my way back up the bank, eyes stretched wide, thinkin' how I can make better time up on the road, maybe get myself down to the place where the creek narrows, and Shiloh might be close enough I can reach out to him somehow.

David's running beside me. I know I'm cryin' but I don't care. One foot squishes every time my shoe hits the pavement. Run as fast as we can.

And then I see this pickup comin' up the road from Friendly, and I'm like to get myself run over.

Judd Travers stops and leans out the window. "You want to get yourself killed?" he calls, right angry. And then, "What's the matter, Marty?" Sees Mr. Ellison comin' up the road behind me, thinks he's chasin' me, maybe. He gets out of the truck.

I'm gasping. Point to the creek.

"Shiloh! He's in the water, and we can't reach him!"

"Marty, that dog will have to get himself out!" Mrs. Ellison calls from far behind us. "Don't you try to go after him, now."

But Judd crashes through the trees and brush, half sliding down the muddy bank, and I point to the head of my beagle back upstream, out there bobbing around in the current. Once, it looks like he goes under. Now David's cryin', too, squeaky little gasps.

Judd don't say a word. He's scramblin' up the bank again and grabs that rope in his pickup. Hobbles down the road, fast as his two bum legs will carry him, goin' even farther downstream, me and David at his heels. Then he ties one end of that rope to a tree at the edge of the water, the other end around his waist, taking his time to make a proper square knot, and I'm thinkin', Don't worry about knots, Judd—just go!

He's plunging into that cold water—all but his boots, which he leaves by the tree. I see now why he went so far downstream, 'cause if we were back closer to the bridge, Shiloh would have gone past us by now.

Another car stops up on the road. I hear voices.

"What happened?"

"Who's out there?"

And Mr. Ellison's giving the answers: "Judd Travers is going after Marty Preston's dog."

Mrs. Ellison and the girls have reached the spot now. Dara Lynn is dripping water, but she won't hear of going home. Every muscle in my body is straining to keep me as close to the water as I can get, my eyes trained on that muddy yellow surface, looking for Shiloh. Maybe this was a mistake. Maybe I should have stayed back where we saw him last, kept my eye on where he went. What if he's pulled under? What if his strength just gave out, and he can't paddle no more?

David gives a shout. We can see Shiloh now. Looks for a time like he's found something to crawl up on out there in that water, a tree limb or something, but while we watch, he's swept away again.

Judd's treading water out in the center of Middle Island Creek, fighting the current himself, and Shiloh's about twenty feet upstream from him. But then—as I stare—I see him turning away from Judd! I wonder if my dog knows how much danger he's in. Wonder if he figures that between the water and Judd Travers, he'll take the water.

"Here, Shiloh! Come here, boy!" Judd calls, his hair all matted down over his eyes.

Shiloh seems spooked. He's lookin' straight ahead, neither to the right nor left. I see his eyes close again, the way he looks lyin' by the stove at night when he's about to fall asleep.

Judd's working his way out farther and farther, trying to get out in the middle of the creek before Shiloh goes by. He's got his head down now, his arms slicing through the water, but it seems like for every three strokes he takes forward, the creek carries him one stroke sideways.

"Don't give up, Shiloh!" I breathe. And then I begin yelling his name. "Come on, Shiloh! Go to Judd. Come on, boy! Come on!"

I wonder if Judd can make it in time. What if Shiloh's too far out and sails on by? What if the rope's not long enough for Judd to reach him? My breath's coming out all shaky.

Judd's out now about as far as he can go, and that rope is stretched taut. One hand is reaching way out, but seems like Shiloh's still trying to paddle away.

"No, Shiloh!" I plead.

Just then Judd gives this whistle. I know that when Shiloh was his, he was taught to come when Judd whistled. Come or else.

I see my dog start to turn. I see Judd's hand go out, and I hear Judd sayin', "Come on, boy. Come on, Shiloh. Ain't going to hurt you none."

And then . . . then my dog's in his arms, and Judd's shoulders go easy. He is just letting that current swing him on downstream and back to the bank. The rope is holding, and Judd don't have to work much—just let the creek do all the carrying.

I slosh along the bank down to where I can see Judd is headed. The Ellisons are going there, too, and a couple of men up on the road.

"Anybody got a blanket?" I hear someone say.

"I got one in my trunk," a man answers.

Arms are reaching out, hands ready. Somebody puts an old blanket around Judd's shoulders soon as he climbs out.

And now Shiloh's against my chest, his rough tongue licking me up one side of my face and down the other, his little body shaking. With Shiloh in one arm, I reach out and put my other around Judd.

"Thanks," I say, my voice all husky. "Thank you, Judd." I'd say more if I could, but I'm all choked up. I just give him a hug with my one free arm, and strangest of all, Judd hugs me back. It's a sort of jerky, awkward hug, like he hadn't had much practice, but it's a start.

I won't repeat what-all my folks said to us later. Dad does the yelling, Ma the crying, and David's got to sit and listen to the whole thing. That me and David went down to that swollen creek in the first place! That we left the girls alone! That Dara Lynn was reckless enough to climb up on that bridge railing. . . .

"Isn't it enough I have the worst toothache of my life without having to come home and find one of my daughters almost drowned?" weeps Ma.

I keep sayin', "I'm sorry"—David, too—but Dad tells us "sorry" wouldn't bring a dead girl back to life. Neither of 'em says anything about Shiloh. That ain't their worry right now.

Dara Lynn hangs her head like the starch has been knocked out of her. Just sits all quiet by the potbellied stove, arms wrapped around her middle. Becky's on the couch, suckin' her thumb. We are the sorriest-looking family right now, but my dog's safe in my arms, and I can't ask for more. Every time he wriggles to get down, I just hold him tighter, and finally he gives up and lays still, knowin' my arms'll get tired by and by.

Next day, though, after Mr. Howard comes for David, my folks are quiet. Seem like every time they walk by one of us, they squeeze a shoulder or pat a head or stroke somebody's hair.

That night after Becky's had her bath and has gone around givin' everyone her butterfly kiss, battin' her lashes against their cheeks, I go out in the kitchen where Dara Lynn's having her graham crackers and milk, and say, "Well, pretty soon you're goin' to have to be sharing that milk with someone else, you know."

She looks at me suspicious-like. "Why?" she says.

"'Cause we're gettin' another member of the family, that's why."

Dara Lynn's eyes open wide. "Ma's having another baby?"

I laugh. "Not this kind of baby, she ain't. It's gonna be your birthday present from me, Dara Lynn. Somebody brought in a litter of kittens to Doc Collins. You want to come with me some Saturday and pick one out, it's yours."

Dara Lynn leaps off her chair and, with graham cracker crumbs on her fingers, hugs me hard. I hug back—a little jerky and awkward, but it's a start.

Everybody's talkin' about Judd Travers. Michael Sholt thought he was going to have the best story of all—that Halloween dummy he and his cousin dumped in the creek to fool us—but it's Judd everyone wants to hear about.

After David told his dad what had happened, Mr. Howard drove up to Judd's a few days later to write a story about him for the paper. But then, everyone from here to Friendly could tell it—how Dara Lynn fell in the creek, how Shiloh jumped in to save her, and Judd went in for Shiloh.

Asked what he was thinking about out there in that rushing water, Judd said, "Well, I guess I was worried some but I was more scared of not saving Shiloh, on account of that dog once saved me."

Once that newspaper story come out, someone even asked Judd if he'd like to be a volunteer for the Rescue Squad down in Sistersville. He's thinking on it.

We talk about it some in school—how dangerous a flood can get—and on the way home one afternoon, sittin' there beside David Howard, I say, "If you'd asked me last summer if Judd Travers would be a hero, I would have bet my cowboy hat it couldn't happen."

"I'd have bet my new Nikes," says David.

"Not in a million years," I say.

I eat the snack Ma's put out for me, and then—with Dara Lynn and Becky playin' out on the bag swing—I head over to Judd Travers' place. His pickup's not there—he's still at work—but I got a hammer stickin' out of one pocket, pliers and wire clippers out of the other.

His dogs bark like crazy when they see me comin' around the trailer, but they know me now, and I let them sniff my fingers before I unhook that wire fencing and start to work on the gate. Me and Judd almost had it done. I see how he got one of the hinges around that pole, and I set to work on the other. What'll it be like, I'm wondering, not to have to worry anymore about Judd Travers hurting my beagle? To visit him and not have to worry is he drunk? Pretty nice, I reckon.

Gettin' the gate to swing right ain't—isn't—as easy as it seems. You got to get the hinges on straight up and down, or the gate will hang crooked. I see I got the pin shafts turned to one side so the gate's tipped. Got to loosen the bolts and start all over again. But finally, when I give the gate a push, it opens in and it opens out, just the way Judd needs it to do.

I clip off the extra fencing, put it back behind Judd's shed. And then, makin' sure that gate's latched the way it's supposed to be, I go back up the road to where Shiloh's still waiting for me at the bridge. I scoop him up in my arms and let him wash my face good—beagle breath and all.

I'm thinking that someday, maybe, when I cross that bridge and head down this road to Judd's trailer, Shiloh might come along, sure that he's mine forever and nothing's going to change that.

Don't know if a dog—or a man, either—ever gets to the place where he can forget as well as forgive, but enough miracles have come my way lately to make me think that this could happen, too.

The Shiloh Trilogy

by

PHYLLIS
REYNOLDS
NAYLOR

Shiloh

Shiloh Season

Saving Shiloh
